Brooklyn Hei

Critically acclaimed Egyptian author, Miral al-Tahawy was born in Sharqiya in the Egyptian Delta into a Bedouin family of the al-Hanadi tribe. The youngest of seven children, she is now Professor of Arabic at the School of International Letters and Cultures, Arizona State University. Her previous works *The Tent* (1998), *Blue Aubergine* (2002), *Gazelle Tracks* (2008) have collectively been translated into many languages. *Brooklyn Heights* is her fourth novel to be published in English.

9 39831771

Brooklyn Heights

MIRAL AL-TAHAWY

*

Translated by Samah Selim

faber and faber

First published in 2010 as *Bruklin Hayts*
by Merit Publishing House Cairo
This translation first published in Egypt in 2011
by the American University in Cairo Press
First published in this edition by arrangement with the
American University in Cairo Press in 2012
by Faber and Faber Limited
Bloomsbury House, 74–77 Great Russell Street,
London WC1B 3DA

This paperback edition first published in 2013

A CIP record for this book
is available from the British Library

ISBN 978–0–571–28005–6

Flatbush Avenue

She had found it on a Google map of Brooklyn, a narrow strip making its way up towards the long, arching span that connects the two islands. She watches as sparkling new cars zoom across the Brooklyn Bridge, pedestrians stream down the walkway, and tourists admire the setting sun from its heights. They gaze in awe at the tip of Manhattan, which looks from up there like a birthday cake ablaze with candles, a round and luscious apple, brilliant with lit skyscrapers. But she turns her back on the spectacle and heads for Flatbush Avenue, chosen from amongst all those myriad streets because it becomes her: a woman shouldering her solitude, a couple of suitcases, and a child who leans into her whenever he grows tired of walking. She carries a few manuscripts of unfinished stories in a small backpack along with the other important documents: birth and vaccination certificates, residence papers, copies of degrees, employers' letters of recommendation, bank papers, and a signed rental contract for an apartment she's never seen.

All she knows about her new home is that it's located on the corner of Flatbush and Fifth Avenue near a big public garden in the heart of an old Brooklyn neighbourhood called Park Slope. She looks up 'slope' in the dictionary: a rim or bluff – a place of descent. She likes that; somehow it fits. She walks down Flatbush, which extends from the bridge to the eastern borders of Brooklyn, looking for her building. The avenue stretches out before her long and wide, abruptly intersected by other avenues and streets that twist and turn into different numbers and names. She picks her way along it slowly and carefully because it may well take her into the heart of a world with no pity, because she is afraid most of the time, and because she leads a young child by the hand. She lingers in a peaceful plaza where the smells of children and milky coffee waft out from cafés and where dark-skinned nannies push baby carriages with one hand and hold cell phones to their ears with the other, their high-pitched laughter drowning out the whimpers of their trapped, squirming charges. The side streets are full of restaurants and cafés that give off an aura of mellow sophistication with their heavy wooden furniture and faded oil paintings. She walks past streets that exude an evident passion for everything old, a passion that spills into the aroma of coffee, the gleam of thick-framed spectacles, and the rumble of insomniac scribbling. She watches people sprinting down sidewalks in order to lose a few pounds, people walking elegant and spoiled dogs, people lost in deep plotting of some poem or musical score in the final stages of composition, or perhaps just relaxing before a reiki or yoga session.

She's sure now that she has come to the right place. Everything around her invites nostalgia. She is surrounded by people who seem to be busy with some act of cosmic creation. All of them are writers, as she herself dreams of becoming. They carry backpacks stuffed with hopeful manuscripts. They hunt for agents and publishers and court young magazine editors who will discover their talent by chance and review their work in a few favourable, well-placed lines. And so their dreams come true all at once. She feels at home here in this place where, from a distance at least, people seem to reflect her own image. She, too, dreams of writing, but her one collection of poems – 'I Am Like No Other' – is still a sheaf of loose paper stowed away in an old white handbag inherited from her mother.

✳

She is dragging the suitcases up to the entrance of the new building when he suddenly stops and tugs on her hand: 'Can I buy something to eat?' Before she can answer, he runs into the store next door and straight up to the man behind the counter (who is of Yemeni origin, as they will later discover) and says to him with a speed and succinctness in English that astonishes her: 'A toasted bagel with cream cheese and a strawberry-cranberry juice smoothie.' The order sounds as long and as wide as Flatbush Avenue. It takes her a while to parse out each word. She often has trouble understanding his English in these situations and now she is struggling to count out the coins whose value she still hasn't memorised. She carefully searches for the right words to make him see sense and ask her first before ordering things they might not be able to afford, but he barely gives her the chance to finish her sentence.

'Darling, what if Mama doesn't have enough money with her?'

'I just ordered a cheese sandwich and a glass of juice, Mom. What's the big deal?' he replies testily. His sharp retort reduces her to silence, and the bitter memory of the bagel 'incident' will stay with her for a long time after. Flatbush Avenue has many temptations.

The apartment they move into is not sized to fit the boy's

3

dreams either. It is no bigger than a small matchbox with a window looking out onto the street. When he complains, she tries to convince him that she has chosen the nicest view of Brooklyn just for him. She tells him that he can wave from the window to the nice man who runs the Egyptian diner across the street, who is in the habit of sitting outside his restaurant on a large chair between two life-sized painted wooden statues of King Tutankhamun and Queen Nefertiti. Every morning he carries the two statues outside to welcome his customers and every evening she watches him take them back inside when he closes the shop. Of course, neither she nor her son ever dares to pass between those statues because the nice Egyptian sells his sandwiches at ten dollars apiece. They content themselves with watching him open and close from their window on the third floor and smiling at him as he sits between his pharaonic companions.

One day they visit a small, dingy Chinese restaurant for lunch. It is an especially unpleasant meal. They sit for a long time at a rickety table and drink glasses of water from a tin pitcher carelessly placed in front of them. As always she listens as he speeds through his complicated order. His aptitude with menus no longer amazes her. She only watches him as he pronounces the words quickly and with mystifying confidence: 'Vegetarian noodles with black mushrooms and zucchini.' She nods to the waiter in confirmation. The strange words arrive piled up in a large bowl that he digs into irritably, after drenching the contents with soy sauce. She is foolish enough to open up one of the small clear plastic wrappers that contain oddly shaped biscuits and bite into its brittle, tasteless crust. She spits it out quickly.

'What is this?'

The boy giggles furiously. 'You're not supposed to eat it, Mom. You're just supposed to read the fortune inside.'

She is ever eager to read her fortune in anything and everything: horoscopes, tarot and playing cards, sometimes her palm, even her forehead, if she could have found someone who knew how to interpret its mysterious lines, but she would never have thought to discover it written out on a scroll inside a biscuit. She opens it up with the trepidation of a woman about to learn her inexorable destiny. *That which awaits you is no better than that which you have left behind.* She tears up the paper into tiny pieces and throws them into the pitcher of water.

She gets up to leave, and he hurries out behind her.

'Mom, are you angry with me? Did I spend a lot of money, Mom? Are you mad?'

She keeps walking and he runs after her in the direction of the small box that is now their home.

✻

At night she thinks about how she has begun to forget so many things – addresses, events, the whereabouts of documents. She worries that her keen memory is getting mouldy. She, who once believed that forgetting was a great blessing, is now hunted by oblivion, a monstrous shadow.

She tries to remember the shape of her past homes and fails. She knows that the apartment is somewhere that gathers all streets into itself, like a glass box. People look in and see her, she looks out and sees them, jogging, drinking, embracing their lovers. It is

5

a place that confirms her solitude and verifies her talent for escaping. She often takes long walks up and down Flatbush Avenue. She studies the places where others have lived and tries to chart a map with which to replace the memories she has fled, the memories that have left a blank space in their wake.

Lefferts Historic House is close to where they live. She discovers that, long ago, a wealthy Irish landowner by the name of Busch once owned the entire street and all the houses on it. She takes her son by the hand and they go inside. The mansion has been preserved in its original state. It has a large garden that borders Prospect Park. Together they examine the ground-water pump, the tea room and the upper-storey bedrooms, the fireplace and the walls covered with portraits of the owner and his children, their servants and slaves standing behind them in the shadows, polishing the wood floors and pouring tea from silver pots. The servants slept there, in the stables, on piles of straw that have been carefully recreated for visitors.

She inspects a few antique paintings of Brooklyn in the days when it was an island of farmers and a harbour for docking ships: barns full of straw, vast farms and open fields strewn with the ruins of deserted vessels. She thinks about the warren of narrow streets that they call Fort Greene – home to the largest community of African-Americans in Brooklyn. If she were there she would see dark-skinned women sitting on their stoops and chatting together in shrill voices, though she wouldn't understand a word of what they were saying in between the deep-throated laughter that sounds much like her own. They speak at breakneck speed and puff on cigarettes to the strains of loud music coming

through the open windows – music that drifts through a neighbourhood rich with the African caftans, chilli and spices, oils and
perfumes and colourful jewellery of the hot, brown continent that
is also hers.

Night falls and from the apartment she can hear the sound
of exploding fireworks and popping balloons and shouts full of
sudden, cataclysmic enthusiasm in Fort Greene. A deep chant
rumbles along the length of Flatbush Avenue and wakes it from its
slumber. She opens her window, laughing out loud and clapping
her hands like a madwoman. Hundreds of people open their windows to watch the fireworks and those funny balloons with images
of Obama stamped on them floating in from sleepless Red Hook.
After the fireworks, people stream out onto the streets waving old
maps of Brooklyn in the days before the great bridge was built.
In those days the neighbourhood was made up of small wretched
shacks occupied by freed slaves and poor whites looking for work
in the iron foundries and glass factories or working as day labourers in the fields. The big blue signs have been visible everywhere
on the avenues and streets since her arrival: *Change*. She pins a button printed with that word on her chest as a token of her own
soon-to-be-fulfilled dreams. Her son has the same button pinned
to his school bag. They wear them because, like everyone else,
they too crave change, and its sister declaration: *Hope*; words that
make them feel that they have become a part of this map, a part of
its deepest aspirations. Her son emerges from under the blankets
and opens his eyes wide.

'What's going on?'

'Obama won.'

He smiles, then closes his eyes and goes back to sleep while she stays at the window watching the fireworks, the joy, then the fatigue, then the light of dawn breaking on the avenue littered with empty beer bottles. She listens to the noise made by the giant street-cleaning trucks, then the pregnant silence that rises with the sun. A while later the express bus to Manhattan passes under her window. She watches the office workers hurrying to the subway station and breathes in the aroma of coffee drifting out of apartment windows and cafés and doughnut vans. Later that morning he taps her on the shoulder and asks the same question again.

'Did Obama really win, Mom?'

'Yes.'

He trots after her from the small bedroom to the even smaller kitchen and begins to tick off his laundry list of Obama-inspired wishes. She faces him with a grave expression and gives him her undivided attention because he often complains that she ignores him. She nods her head and restricts herself to a single word, 'Yes,' a word he has grown to hate, a meaningless word conveying nothing, but it's the only one she's got these days.

'I've got to tell Obama that a lot of things have to change.'

'Okay.'

The boy picks out his English words with care. 'He has to change the *environment* and the *rain forest* and *go green everywhere* and change Egypt too. Can he do that?'

'Let's hope so. Everything will turn green.'

'Can I be in an election and win like Obama?'

'Anything is possible.'

'And be the President of the *United States?*'

'Anything is possible.'

'Now? *Now?*'

'There's a time and place for everything, my love.'

She feels like she's getting old. She realises that she has been repeating the same resigned, cautious, and ultimately meaningless words her own mother used ad nauseam ('God willing . . . It's all up to Him . . . Who knows? . . . There's a time and place for everything . . .') and that she's beginning to resemble her mother more and more as time goes by, especially after she cut off the long, coal-black hair that now smells of her mother's favourite Japanese dye. Her walk has also taken on the same listless gait that her mother had at the end of a long day; her mother who constantly brandished her dictionary of essential and incontrovertible truths in order to shackle her dreams of becoming an airline hostess, or an astronomer. 'All knowledge belongs to God, dear, and He commands all,' she would laughingly instruct. So she lets the boy write a long letter to Obama. She remembers that she used to write long letters to God. He never once replied, of course, but that didn't stop her from believing that He would make all her dreams come true.

✳

She takes him by the hand and walks. She walks and walks because she has no work and because the apartment she lives in is stifling and because she can't sleep at night and because her buried anxiety gives a frightening cast to the placid expression in her eyes. When they come home at the end of the day he will lie next to her and watch TV and she'll bury her head even deeper under the covers

9

and dream about them; about the life that she can no longer remember, the life that is slipping through her hands.

Her name is Hend but her nicknames were many. She remembers certain ones: 'Gap-tooth', when her milk teeth were falling out; 'Bucky', because of her protruding upper jaw; 'Thumbs', because her hands weren't able to grasp things properly, as hands should. Objects would slip away from her and shatter because her mind was always far away. Those cruel names turned her into an obstinate mule and made her relationship with her mother a living hell. She would brush her hot tears away with a final sob before exploding into the same insistent stream of questions: 'Why don't you love me? Are you really my mother?' Sometimes her anger drove her to excess: 'I hate you, I hate you!' she would scream. Someone would usually intervene at this point to teach her better manners and she always emerged from the subsequent battle with a brand-new set of wounds.

She was never able to beat a prudent retreat from these battles. Her childish insolence and the feeble scratches she meted out were met with a few fierce slaps that made her long, crooked nose bleed. She would run away to hide under the low wooden bed and cry bitter tears. After a while she would stifle her sobs to listen for the approaching click of those dainty feather slippers that she so coveted. From her spot under the bed she would glimpse a shiny red heel and the hem of her mother's lace nightgown. Night would have fallen by then and she would smell the smoke from her father's cigarette as it wafted in from the room next door. After drawn-out negotiations she would emerge from under the bed, her mother's arm reaching out to smooth her hair and draw her close ('Come here, princess, come to me'), but Hend would resist, gnawing her lip and brushing away the last traces of her tears and whimpering, 'You don't love me.' She remembers her mother hugging her tight. 'Are you crazy? How can a mother not love her daughter? You're the most precious thing in the world to me.' In a flash of clarity, those wistful words reveal to Hend the true extent of their shared despair.

In spite of all of the attempts to break her in, Hend never managed to become the gentle and obedient girl capable of thriving in a jungle of men that her mother hoped and prayed for; all the meticulous and chary instructions ('You're a girl, how will you manage to survive with that stubborn head of yours?') didn't do a bit of good. After all those years, after learning the meaning of suspicion and jealousy and desertion, she now understood that the woman forever pacing the living room in a honey-coloured robe was her twin. They both had the same long nose, worn down by endless nights of crying. She recalled her mother's habit of clutching at her lower back to soothe the chronic pain left behind by many childbirths. She would apply one hot water bottle after another to still the ache while she waited long into the night for Hend's father to come home – if he bothered to come home at all. She refused to believe the many stories that the servants told her about her husband, and the dark circles under her bloodshot eyes told a story of their own in the morning.

Hend knew that if her mother woke up in one of those states a domestic volcano was sure to erupt and that, as the only daughter, she would be its first victim. She would scurry back to her place under the bed yet again, whimpering and listening for the torrent of threats to smash in her stubborn head. She wasn't an entirely innocent party in these battles, for she was more than capable of challenging her mother with her defiant, intimidating eyes. She was also quite good at single-handedly provoking her anger by poking through her private things – her make-up cases and bits of paper carefully shut away in drawers, like the clippings that her mother collected from *Your Personal Doctor* and *Eve* and a host of other magazines specialising in domestic and marital problems. There were articles about how to monopolise your husband's love by putting perfume in your bathwater and sweet-smelling mastic in the folds of your underwear, or how to make sticky caramelised sugar paste to depilate unsightly body hair. She devoured all this in an excess of curiosity, not paying the slightest attention to her mother's warnings. The only thing that saved her from her mother's wrath was that she was a model student. Hend's mother took comfort in the hope that her daughter would make something of herself someday, perhaps by getting an education. In the meantime she didn't bother to hide her anxiety about Hend's future and would often remind her that she was not pretty and therefore shouldn't count on her looks to get her through life. It didn't help that she was no good at housekeeping and so God only knew who would be willing to marry her.

But Hend did find a husband, at least for a few years. She had a baby, she sprinkled perfume on her pillowcases, she kept her supple skin smooth and inviting. She diligently followed all the instructions that she had pored over as a young girl, in articles with titles such as 'How to ward off marital boredom and keep your husband by frequently changing the colour of your underwear' and 'Learning the difference between acceptable and unacceptable jealousy'. But all these recipes led to the same dead end that her mother had long ago predicted. The simple fact was that she was 'no good', and that she didn't understand the first thing about life or men.

The history of that short-lived marriage was summed up in an endless string of domestic spats involving slamming doors and hurtful expressions. These verbal skirmishes evolved soon enough into packed suitcases and copious tears and neighbours spying and friends intervening. That was when a simple truth, clear as the light of day, gradually dawned on her: one of them had to choose the best way out.

One morning, her husband took a shower, splashed on his favourite cologne, carefully chose a pair of white cotton boxer shorts still soft and velvety like a first night of passion, stuffed a pair of black silk pyjamas and some condoms into his briefcase, then walked out the door and never came back. A few months later, Hend put everything that still belonged to her into a few suitcases, covered the furniture in plastic sheeting, and left with her bags in tow. From her husband she inherited a visa for the US, a child, and two suitcases containing the smallest and lightest of his toys. And this was how they ended up in a tiny apartment on the corner of Flatbush and Fifth. Her father used to say, 'Whatever the north wind brings, the south wind takes away.' And here she stands now, wretched and alone, in a place where the four winds mightily converge. The women around her – some younger, most older – who come from all over God's mysterious lands look exactly like herself in ways that are painful, frightening, and comforting at the same time. Every day she crosses Grand Army Plaza to go to the subway station or the Public Library. She likes to go to the Library to look at the pictures of famous writers whose ranks she dreams of joining. They comfort her high up there on the walls, because they, like her, one day discovered that life is not beautiful. She moves past Hemingway's portrait and shyly sits down next to some people who seem much more at ease than herself. Above the table there is a poster with the words 'Learn English' printed on it. Next to the poster hangs a black-and-white photograph of Albert Einstein, underneath which is written, 'Einstein was a refugee too.'

'My name is Hend. I came here from Cairo — why, I don't exactly know. I'm trying to learn English. I love the Arabic language. I used to be an Arabic teacher. I feel really shy whenever I have to speak in English. Even the words I've learned properly I seem to pronounce in a way that no one can understand. I like to go to places where cultured people gather, and I pretend to be one of them though I don't really understand what they are talking about. I sit on a chair in a far corner so that no one bothers to ask me anything and I don't feel the need to say anything. The expression, "Excuse me, what did you say?" which I hear all the time, makes me freeze. I have a serious problem communicating with people. I know that Pluto is in the House of Capricorn — meaning in the seventh house opposite Cancer. This is the house of tolerance and compassion. Maybe that's the reason people don't understand me — because the opposing energy of Pluto is facing my zodiac sign. I feel my stupidity and ignorance more than at any other time in my life. I feel that I have to re-think so many things.'

The others introduce themselves simply and clearly.

'Fatima from Mali. Twenty-four years old. I grew up in France. I came here to visit family. I'm a salesgirl in a store.'

'Faridnaz, Pakistan. Twenty-two. Recently married. I came here to join my husband.'

'Alejandro from Peru. I'm a building superintendent.'

'Nazahat. I'm from Bosnia. I used to be a doctor. I'm fifty-five.'

'My name is Dawij. I come from Haiti. I'm eighteen years old. I clean houses.'

'Said. My name is Said. I'm an Egyptian Copt. I'm a limousine driver.'

They always change. Some come and some vacate their places for new ones to come. After class, they peddle cosmetics and cleaning detergents. The informal introductions are always much simpler. With her they exchange truncated sentences, as though she were an outsider, not belonging. Some of them ask her in bad Arabic: 'Is you Muslim?' She nods her head happily, longing for connection, a few friendships or acquaintances to pass into her life. She talks about her country and tries to pinpoint its location for them somewhere between Israel and Mecca – those two poles of strategic interest in the region. She is forced to show her own ignorance when she asks about the location of Haiti or Peru. In the end, they exchange the useful titbits of information gleaned by exiles and immigrants: the best places to shop cheaply, job openings, where to find soup kitchens and welfare offices, rental prices for apartments or single rooms, and short, cheap excursions to places like Sheepshead Bay near the end of the subway line, where the exiles sit on benches by the sea that reminds them of other ports and waterways. They spend the endless time on their hands fishing in the ocean that separates them from their homelands. They watch the passing ships and gaze at the Statue of Liberty in the distance, the Verrazano Bridge, and the contours of New Jersey. They smoke cigarettes and talk about the motherland and things like visas and health insurance and social security.

In class she gets to know a lot of Arabs who have recently arrived from Morocco and Algeria, Sudan and Yemen. They never speak to her in Arabic: 'I speak colloquial,' they say, if she tries to draw them into conversation. They chatter together in bad English and claim that they know next to nothing about each other's countries because the Arab world is so big and wide and very different. She tries to believe this, and she tells them that she's an Arabic teacher, that Arabic is an endangered language, a language that is slowly dying out, but she clings to it because, unfortunately, she tends to get insanely attached to things and love defies forgetfulness.

She clutches her papers and crosses Flatbush, talking to herself. She often talks to herself in that obscure, whispered, endangered language that makes passers-by stare at her. She sits on the wooden bench in front of her son's school, sipping coffee, smoking a cigarette, and waiting for him to come out. The cold pierces her to the bone and the cigarette doesn't warm her up. She muses on the cold piling up in layers around her face, turning her into a tired, autumnal woman, a woman naked and alone who resembles no one. He comes towards her slowly, gingerly, and he doesn't kiss her. He gently puts his hand in her hand and they walk side by side, keeping pace. Mother and son are almost the same height. He startles her with questions to which she has no answers.

'Mom, you didn't do your hair.'

'What do you mean?'

'You look strange these days. Why don't you put make-up on any more?'

'Maybe I don't have time.'

'You just don't care how you look.'

'The important thing is that I care about you. What did you do today?'

'We had a demonstration and we made signs saying *Change*, and we had a food strike.'

'Why?'

'The food in the school cafeteria is awful. Every day it's the same thing. So we all complained and we wrote a letter saying that we want pizza and hamburgers and ice-cream instead, and we waved pictures of Obama with *Change* written on them. You have to change too, Mom.'

'How?'

'Your hair, for example. The way you look. You know . . .'

'So you don't like your mother any more?'

'No, it's just that you have to change. You're always sad. *Sad*,' he repeated in English.

'Okay.'

'But Mom?'

'Yes?'

'When you change the way you dress and everything, you have to promise me that you won't love anyone else. You can go out with your friends and have fun – you know, you can *hang out* with them.'

'Fine.'

'But if one of your friends asks you to go out on a *date*, you have to say no. *Date* means you have to get married and stuff, and I don't want you to love anyone else.'

'Fine.'

'I'll always keep on loving you, but in *high school* I might start doing dates and go out with a *girlfriend!*'

'Okay, when we get to high school we'll figure it out.'

'But I'll never ever leave you, and I'll always visit you. You can even live with me when you get old and stuff.'

'Of course. I'll get old and wrinkly and die.'

'But I don't want you to get old.'

'. . .'

'Or die.'

'Alright, then, I won't.'

2

Bay Ridge

Flatbush Avenue is crossed by many streets. She travels the vast length of Flatbush alone because for the longest time she was too shy to go into any of the many Arab cafés and restaurants by herself. She takes him by the hand and walks along the boardwalk, watching the small ferries crossing the Narrows. She walks till she can no longer feel her feet moving. She wants to get rid of those extra pounds and the din of the thoughts crowding and jostling in her head.

'I know this street by heart,' he says in a thin, irritable voice. 'I don't want to go to Bay Ridge again. *Please.*'

She can't leave him at home by himself and he can't keep up with her long, hurried strides for miles on end. Sometimes he insists on staying home: 'I don't want to go to Bay Ridge!' And when he does go with her, the sacrifice is inevitably tied to a long list of demands: 'If I go with you, can I . . . ? Can I buy . . . ? Can I have . . . ?' The older he gets, the more he reminds her of his father. The older he gets, the more she begins to realise that they are each moving in opposite directions, and that she will have to let go soon.

On her way to Bay Ridge, she passes through many different ethnic neighbourhoods. There's the Mexican area, where doors are never shut fast and people sell home-made ice-cold drinks from hospitable stoops. The women have skin the colour of wheat and thick black hair like her own. They cross the threshold of middle age in bright colourful clothing that bares their full, sated breasts. Playing children dart and weave around them. She watches the unemployed day labourers standing in groups on the wide sidewalks, waiting for work with tool kits in hand – ropes, bits of iron, small axes, garden shears. Rough hands and sturdy muscles ready to carry and move and fix just about anything. They look a lot like the day labourers she used to see scattered in squares and on the narrow sidewalks of her own country. They too wait patiently for small jobs that may or may not material-ise. They sit here and there in circles, rubbing their rough hands in slow, relaxed, almost ritual motions, sharing cigarettes and coffee and cheap street-food, staring down the unknown with fierce, defiant eyes. She's afraid of these gatherings, which are al-ways pregnant with the possibility of sudden, mysterious fights breaking out, trivial skirmishes with passers-by, or conspiratorial whispers that end in heckling a passing woman like herself with the short dark hair of their sisters, and a child in tow.

On her walk she passes the cemetery that sits on top of a hill and looks down upon a huge church. She is fond of the plaster virgins that stand in front of the houses of this neighbourhood. She feels that she herself is frozen, like them, in some dimension or other, with that same expression of martyrdom. She likes the atmosphere of the cemetery and the colourful bouquets of plastic flowers. She likes to see the old women sitting in rocking chairs on their porches. Their friendly greetings always take her by sur-prise. The Latin neighbourhood is much gayer. Beautiful mulatto women noisily bustle around houses whose front rooms have been turned into small restaurants. In the evening many of them are transformed into schools or dance halls for salsa and tango. The smell of the great trade in temporary joy wafts out from around them: music, warm bars, the dancers vying to demonstrate their talent, and the scent of intoxicating green smoke drifts through the places of buying and selling.

She's never had the chance to linger into the night there. He always pulls at her clothes to drag her away as though in fear of the spectacle of bodies coming close together in the dance. He would pull her by the hand in the direction of the bus stop and then begin his interrogation.

'Mom, do you love me?'

'Of course.'

'And you'll never leave me?'

'Never.'

'Okay, let's go home.'

✻

Her father's house was like no other house. As a child, Hend would wander around the village and peer at the dark clay houses that opened onto long corridors and narrow alleys. Their roofs were made of straw piled in high mounds and the walls were left unpainted. Through the open doors she could see interior courtyards and cowsheds, or large ceramic urns and clay braziers with a teapot or a few potatoes perched in their smoky bellies. On cold nights, cats – and sometimes people – would climb up to sleep on the warm stone ledges of these ovens. The doors of all the houses around stood open to her gaze. On her walk, she could see all their nooks and crannies: the plastic bamboo mats for sitting and sleeping, the noisy play of children, men and women gathered in the rituals of dispute and forgiveness.

The streets were dry and dusty in the summer and full of sticky mud in the winter. She walked along them on her daily trip to the mosque and she watched the women pour the dirty washing water out in front of their houses. The smell of cooking wafted out from kerosene stoves, and the smell of dung and laundry detergent filled the air. In the mosque's interior courtyard she contemplated the tall eucalyptus tree that stood next to the wooden bier on which the dead were washed in preparation for burial. She passed the power station, the municipal registry of births, and the local threshing machine. She heard the loud rhythmic sound of the gears grinding in its guts, and the clamour of the women crowding around it. She passed the village's only public drinking-water faucet, fixed above its stone basin. On her way to the Muqawi Primary School, she saw lots of things.

She is certain now that their house was not like any of the other houses. Her father's house was surrounded by a sturdy mud wall covered with coloured chalk pictures of camels, litters, and caravans travelling to Mecca with drawn curtains. The drawings, smudged now by rain, were a record of her family's descent from a tribe of grandfathers whose ancestors bestowed the precious linen cloth from the Land of the Copts upon the sacred Ka'ba. They were meant to bear witness to the long-ago voyage of a pilgrim who had saddled his camels, gathered his men, and ridden the sea to cross over to those blessed shores, and then safely returned from the land of God's chosen prophet. In the middle of the wall stood a huge gate, once stately and imposing but now battered by time and patched up with wooden planks. Inside the walls, an avenue of eucalyptus and flame trees led to a number of small, adjoining clay rooms. An old Cadillac inhabited one of them and the others were all empty like abandoned train cars. The grandfather's wives were once housed in those rooms – the pure-bred Arab Bedouin woman, the noblewoman descended from the Prophet's line, and the Coptic wife. Her father inherited these structures, like everything else, from his father, and the empty clay rooms were eventually used to store grain and feed. It was the ideal spot for games of hide-and-seek. Her mother sent the children to play there whenever visitors came.

Their house was not beautiful. A flight of steps ascended to a large balcony that led in turn to a vast, bare reception room, empty of furniture because 'furniture is so easily broken'. Her mother would spread a rush mat on the floor in the summer and a woven wool carpet in the winter. In this wide-open space the children ate and ran around and did battle. With the seasons the family moved from the western balcony to the eastern balcony and from the summer room to the winter room. The reception room was usually reserved for guests, and the door to her father's room was always shut fast.

Her mother would sit on the balcony and dream of a new house like the many-storeyed houses of the village with commanding views of the world inside and out. She once plucked up her courage and told her husband of her dreams: 'I wish I could live in a house like that of my noble uncle Lamlum.' Her father, who had just taken

23

the last sip of his bottle of beer, twirled his moustache ironically and replied, 'God bless him, my dear. He's the son of Bedouins just like us – or was he born with the mark of prophecy on his shoulder?' Her mother, who usually avoided talking about her distant uncles, turned her face away from him in silent anger.

Just once, upon the death of the uncle in question, she took Hend with her on a trip to that faraway house. Her mother spent half that memorable day washing, ironing, and brushing her black mourning clothes, and rummaging through her remaining jewels and perfumed handkerchiefs in musty drawers. In a picture-perfect image, like a photograph preserved in an old family album, she turned to adjust her husband's tie as Hend stood watching in her crisp blue dress and shiny white ribbons.

The old Cadillac carried them through vast expanses of sandy land on the edges of Buhaira province. Hend's grandmother, the Sharifa, was very fat and white. She placed a pinch of snuff in her nostrils and sneezed into an embroidered white handkerchief. She wiped away the tears with real feeling, shaking her head in a movement that signified her resignation to God's will. Hend's mother sat opposite her, stiff and elegant, and cried a little. She exchanged kisses with young women dressed in black, plunged into conversation on subjects near and far. Her mother's nose coloured slightly as she carefully inspected the jewellery, the elegant clothes, the sheer stockings, and the brass coffee-pots around her, and inhaled the pungent smell of Meccan incense perfuming the air. She finished her cup of coffee, kissed the hand of the noble grandmother with deliberate emotion, and took her leave. For a long time after this visit, the father avoided upsetting her. When she boasted about her dead aristocratic uncles, he would reply with feeling, 'God have mercy on us all.'

Their house was not many-storeyed as her mother fervently wished it to be. The floor of the eastern balcony was covered in polished black and white tiles like a chess board. Hend drew a hopscotch grid on it with chalk. Sometimes the children used it to mark out opposing goalposts for soccer matches or invisible corners for hide-and-seek and games of Blind Bear. A heavy door inlaid with a pair of stained-glass windows stood in the middle of the house. The cracked glass panels were criss-crossed with tracks of white solder. The door was very heavy and difficult to open and close. It was repeatedly subjected to fierce slammings that inevitably produced more cracks in the glass. The delicate coloured glass tended to shatter whenever an angry hand chanced to fall upon it; her father's hand in particular would make it shudder and splinter whenever he slammed it behind him, cursing the wretched day on which he was born. Afterwards, Hend would discover her mother curled up tight into a shaking, weeping ball.

Other kinds of tremors often assailed that unfortunate door: the shrill shouts of playing children running to catch balls that invariably overshot their mark and crashed into the glass. Each of the five boys had left his mark on the walls and windows of the chaotic house, as they had done collectively on their besieged mother's body. Her father's room, however, was the exception to the rule. It was always quiet and tidy. No one dared to open its door unless their father was stretched out on his bed, reading the papers, his wife sitting on a chair at his side in her sesame and honey-coloured robe printed with red flowers, talking calmly.

Hend would be playing somewhere or other, her ear cocked to catch the tone of his voice. If it was clear and full of laughter, spring would come to caress their glass door. Mother smiled happily and didn't scold, even when Hend covered her face in flour to scare her brothers, or climbed all the way up the flame tree in a monkey-jump contest, or poured a whole bottle of lavender cologne on her chest before poking through the powders and lotions on her mother's dressing table.

Hend would collect handfuls of sandy earth and stones and bits of old toys and empty bottles so that she could play her favourite game – Little House. On the dusty ground she would draw the outlines of a house, with kitchen and bedroom and children. She would put her rag-doll child on her lap and feed it milk from her breast. She would sweep dust from the corners of her imaginary house, a house whose windows were always caressed by spring, a house in which she could drift off to sleep untroubled by the dark shadow of a man shouting at a woman dressed in a robe the colour of honey and sesame seeds: 'I'll go to hell and you'll never see me again! Do you think you can tie me down with a pile of children?' In other nightmares he would drag the woman along by the embroidered border of her honey-coloured robe and say to her: 'Get out! That's it. I don't want you any more!'

Hend knew that the heavy thud of groans and kicks coming from behind the door would surely shatter its coloured glass panels. Her mother always emerged from these battles with exhausted, swollen eyes. The next morning she bound the door's wounds with plastic strips to stop the cold winter wind from coming in through the cracks.

The gate of her father's house was huge and ancient. One day, long ago, the camel caravans had gone out through that entrance and had never returned. She would often contemplate it from the inside, ponder the movement of the universe from behind it. The gaiety of passers-by, the screams of children she didn't know, a ball made of stuffed socks that was passed between the nimble feet of running boys. Sometimes, in spite of the threats, she would open it cautiously, or creep underneath it. She would steal glances at the girls who looked nothing like her. They played out there, on open ground. Then one of her brothers saw her dawdling outside and pulled her away by her hair. Her mother threatened her: 'I'll break your legs if you cross the threshold again.' So from then on she could only look at the dividing line and swallow her want till the day when she too could step over to the other side and never return.

Hend would watch the gypsies pass through in springtime. They would stream by in front of the gate and their animals kick up a cloud of dust behind them. She would wander in the space behind their tents pitched on the banks of the Abbasiya Canal. She dreamt of a house that would hug the street to itself, a house whose insides she could see without having to knock, a house with a wide hospitable courtyard to invite the greetings of passers-by, a house across whose open threshold floated the smell of cooking, of washing and the sweat of strangers. But the gate of her father's house was high and shut fast. She would stand staring at it, and it would stare back at her.

*

Hend walks along the endless streets of Brooklyn. She never gets tired of walking in this land, alone and anonymous. She passes through Latino and Italian neighbourhoods and arrives in the Asian neighbourhood where she likes to shop for fruit and vegetables. She compares prices in the cheaper Vietnamese markets. She passes through the Turkish neighbourhood and continues on to Bay Ridge. She is amazed at how the architecture, the people's faces and their skin colour, the merchandise and the wafting cooking smells are all so different. By now she will have walked for more than seventy blocks. By now she will have grown weary of the cacophony of languages and loud music and she will begin to long for the sweet aroma of water pipes. She heads for a small local coffee shop. The men inside flash curious smiles at her. Their good-natured dirty jokes remind her of home. Here is the Arab world in microcosm – the Brooklyn Gulf. They come from Gaza and Nablus, Beirut and Alexandria. The old men of the first generation stretch out in their wooden chairs and curse their exile as they nibble on sweet Arab pastries from The Groom's Sweets next door. Through the window she watches old men come in and out of the storefronts: Seaside Fish, Abu Ali's Falafel, Friendship Kushari, and Abu Kamal's Grocery, which sells halal meat. Old photographs hang in the windows of the Arab shops as well as maps of antique cities and signs proclaiming solidarity with the suffering people of Gaza and South Lebanon. The residents spill joyfully out onto the streets when the Egyptian soccer team score three goals against Brazil, even though they lose the match. They pour insults on FIFA in a myriad of dialects.

The coffee shop she likes to go to is called Arabian Nights.

It's small and dark and the hookahs smell of stale water. The first time she stepped inside, she sniffed the air slowly and cautiously. She glanced around her stealthily and realised that she was the only woman in the place, so she sat down and started leafing through some newspapers and yellowed magazines. The waiter was tall and skinny. He reminded her of one of her Arabic-language teachers at school. The clients called him 'sir' out of affection but also, as she discovered later, as a mark of respect for his mysterious past. She tried to hide her face behind the newspaper but he accosted her with pointed questions nonetheless.

'Do you live alone?'

'Yes.'

'Have you found a job yet?'

'Luckily, yes.'

'So I guess you have a visa.'

'I have a residence permit.'

'You mean a Green Card?'

'No. I'm a school teacher.'

The waiter to whom she was lying was called Muhammad, and he kept asking her questions she didn't know how to answer. In Bay Ridge, they kill the heavy time on their hands by inventing ingenious questions designed to expose the white lies of newcomers; immigrants like themselves looking for a visa, a job, and a room. Muhammad continued his interrogation.

'What do you teach?'

'Arabic.'

'You think Arabs in America need to learn Arabic? Now they're bringing teachers over here?'

'. . .'

'So, you're working?'

'I've got papers.'

'Does it put bread on the table?'

'Sometimes.'

'Look, consider me a brother. Forget the visa and the teaching and all that stuff. If you need a job just say so. I'll be right here. I've been here for fourteen years.'

'Alright.'

'I've got a BA in business administration. I used to dream of being a merchant sailor. You see what I do now.'

'Yes, I can see.'

'You don't like to talk much. It's obvious.'

She nodded her head slightly and said, 'Sometimes.'

He looked as though he was finally on the point of giving up. He was puzzled by this woman who had come in by herself and was sitting by herself and seemed to be afraid of opening up, talking about any old thing or making up stories, like the others do to give their lives some meaning.

'Okay, then,' he said glumly. 'If you need something, just holler.'

'Thanks,' she answered curtly, which seemed to annoy him even more.

She watched the marijuana smoke spiralling up and wreathing the TV screen, which was showing a soccer match. The game drew a slew of crude comments: your mother, your sister, the whore that you married, any excuse for exchanging friendly insults. A man came up and introduced himself, taking a seat at her table as he munched on a piece of sweet pastry. From his accent she could tell that he was from Iraq. He told her that he was the first of the lot to arrive in Bay Ridge but that he couldn't quite remember the exact number of years. He wiped away a piece of kunafa stuck to his lip and his sharp, thin smile made him look like an eagle just before it swoops down on its prey. The deep purple circles under his eyes made her wonder whether he might be an alcoholic despite his constant chatter about the Islamic Center on the corner of Fulton Street and MacDougal. He questioned her in the same familiar and slightly suspicious tone as Muhammad the waiter.

'Are you married?'

She inclined her head ambiguously, so he launched into the second question.

'Do you have children?'

'A boy,' she replied.

Abd al-Karim was a Kurd, and he seemed nicer than he looked. He smiled again and started to give her advice. 'Children are the most important thing in the world. Life here is hard. You have to keep a constant eye on your kids.'

He finally got up and went back to his interrupted game of dominoes. Later, when she had gotten to know the café and its clients a bit better, she learned that Abd al-Karim was part of the first wave of refugees to come to New York from Iraq and that he married a Mexican girl called Jojo. Jojo used to work in a coffee shop in Brighton Beach. She was dark-skinned and voluptuous, all silky flesh and curves, made for love. Hend wondered whether Abd al-Karim himself, with his thick moustache and his unusual tallness, used to be attractive in some long-ago time. The couple rented a small apartment in Brighton Beach because Jojo felt more comfortable living in a mixed Russian–Italian neighbourhood rather than an Arab one. She loved the ocean, the cosy local bars, the stout Russian men who looked a little like her husband. She claimed that their tough exteriors hid big hearts; men who turned into fragile, suffering creatures after their first drink. She confessed that she had had affairs while Abd al-Karim was out driving his taxi day and night, and she would complain bitterly about the strong smell of arak that always clung to her ex-husband.

She ended the marriage pretty quickly after their third daughter was born, but he didn't move out because he had nowhere else to go. Besides, he wanted to stay close to the girls, who were growing up fast. He watched this happen with mounting anxiety. His oldest daughter, Diana, was beginning to look just like her mother, slender, voluptuous, and alluring, the exquisite fruit of mixed parentage. She took after her mother in many ways. She was shameless and defiant and full of teeming life. She was also brutally honest to the point of insolence. No one but her Creator could control her, as Abd al-Karim was in the habit of saying. She had inherited the hated dark circles under his eyes and she waged constant war on them with concealers and creams. Like her mother, she was obsessed with the arts of the body — massage therapy, moisturisers, and face masks — and she loved being photographed in provocative poses. Abd al-Karim beat her ferociously sometimes, or else he smashed the furniture in the apartment, and picked fights for the most trivial reasons. After these fits, Jojo always kicked him out of the house and filed restraining orders with the police. He would have ended up in jail on a number of occasions if not for the intervention of the people at the Islamic Center, who patiently talked to him about cultural differences and did the best they could to put out the fire burning in his heart.

He finally moved out of the Brighton Beach apartment and into Bay Ridge, and he began to spend all his free time sitting in the coffee shop and talking endlessly to anyone who would listen about the dangers of raising children in this hell of a place. In spite of his partiality to drink, he started to visit the Islamic Center regularly. He liked to sit and talk with the imam of the mosque and would sometimes even run little errands for him. He began to do volunteer work for the Center; he specialised in making funeral arrangements with the Muslim Cemetery in New Jersey for people from the community. He was the one who bought the white cloth for the shrouds, the incense, and anything else the family needed. Sometimes other volunteers would pile into his car and they would drive behind the hearse to the cemetery, where prayers would call on God to raise the departed soul to His eternal Paradise and to forgive the body about to be buried in a non-Muslim land. Newly arrived refugees went to him for advice about where to go shopping or where to find housing or Arab cafés and restaurants and how to guard children from the corruption of their new home ('God have mercy on us all'). Abd al-Karim was also a firm believer in the Twin Towers conspiracy theory circulated in an anonymous letter that instructed the receiver to copy it and send it on to the largest number of people possible ('so that God may multiply your good deeds'). The letter explained the miracle of the Quran and how it had predicted the events of September 11 and the destruction of the Cities of Injustice.

Hend sits by herself opposite Abd al-Karim, who hands her a new piece of paper every time he sees her; a piece of paper that, as always, she has no desire to read. She smokes her water pipe and gazes at the faces of the regular clients. When she senses that another argument is about to erupt, she decides to leave. She buys a pack of cigarettes and sits on a bench by the seaside, watching the sun as it sinks into the vast Atlantic, then she takes the bus back home.

Always, when nostalgia, loneliness, or self-loathing pulls her back to Bay Ridge, her son categorically refuses to go with her.

'I don't want to go to that place.'

'Why not?'

'It's dirty. And it's *vulgar*,' he moans in English. 'I don't want to be one of them.'

'We can eat some Egyptian noodles.'

'I don't want to!' he bawls hysterically.

'Are you going to make Mama go alone?'

'Why do you like it so much?'

'Maybe because it reminds me of home.'

'But I don't like Bay Ridge! And I don't want to go back to Egypt either.'

3

The Green Cemetery

Seventh Avenue is divided by Greenwood Cemetery, which sits on a hill that reminds her of Pharaoh's Hills back home. She likes to wander its winding avenues early in the morning because of the flowers, and because of the profound silence that used to frighten her. She passes the time reading the names of the dead who lie beneath the marble slabs. The elation of death and oblivion, the peacefulness of old people, wash over her. The houses that face the cemetery are also old, with stiff marble facades. Elderly Russian and Hispanic women sit in wooden rocking chairs on their porches. The Latino ladies carefully step out of gaily coloured houses into the pale winter sunlight, houses that put the grey hues of other neighbourhoods to shame. They smile at her like children. She smiles back and walks on with leaden, worried steps, as though she were approaching an ending of some kind. The sturdy coat that she bought at a thrift store smells of mothballs and mould. It weighs on her body, heavy and forlorn. She disappears inside it, seamlessly blending into her surroundings: the old women and the streets, cold, solitary, neutral.

She has become more like her grandmother than her mother, she thinks to herself. She remembers how she used to squirm in her grandmother's lap, an angry child with a naked bottom. She was hard to keep up with as a child, light and thin, teething and crawling and speaking well before any of her brothers did. She proved that she was a creature capable of surviving and flourishing on the barest necessities of life. Her mother often left her to her own devices. She would crawl up the hill behind the western balcony right up to the solitary room roofed in wood and clay that looked, for all the world, like a heavenly dome. They called it 'the high place'. A woman sat at its door, a woman who they did not call 'grandmother' but rather 'the Guest', though she never once stepped out of the confines of the family home. 'The Guest is sleeping,' they would say, or, 'The Guest wants such-and-such,' or, 'Go and bring the buttermilk pan from the Guest's room.'

The Guest was a tiny, timid peasant woman with a green tattoo on her chin. The back of her hand was also covered with tattoos – a bride, a fish, and a lion. Her room always smelled of perfumed candles. She wove rope out of long strands of fibre and mended the holes in old clothes. Her dresses too were embroidered with tiny lions and fishes and dolls. Little Hend would crawl after her mother for half the day, crying and trying to catch hold of the hem of her long robe: 'Mama sit. Mama *dees*' (Mama sit down so I can nurse). And because her mother was constantly running around taking care of the housework, she would always send her to the Guest's room. The Guest had no work to keep her busy. She would take the squirming Hend into her lap and stroke her back until she fell asleep. Or she would teach her how to stretch out her hand and feed the chicks and the baby ducklings with the leftovers from a carton. When the Guest died, they prayed for her soul: 'Her hand was blessed . . . May God have mercy on her,' adding, 'if she bore witness to the One God before the Angel came to take her away.'

Said her mother: 'Your grandfather Muqawi was big and strong and bedded both slave and freewoman, Arab and non-Arab. But the peasant girl from the Coptic Estate – she was the only one who bore him children. May God rest her soul, if she truly testified before the Angel came for her.'

And this was how Hend came to understand – after the Angel of Death had swept through their house – that the woman who had lived in that solitary room was her grandmother; a small peasant woman who came from the Coptic Estate, or 'the White Estate' in the days before the Nur Mosque (as the people called it), with its enormous marvel of a marble dome, had been built. She was a young girl with the ragged cloth belt of impoverished agricultural day labourers tied around her waist. One day the Chief of Bedouins with his regal headdress passed through the fields on his stallion and saw the delicate white flowers of the cotton plant blooming from that belt. He looked at the girl's belly, puffed up with cotton blossoms, and straight away divined the auspicious signs of a fertile seed. 'She will surely be the mother of a male child,' he said to himself. 'The Prophet himself – peace and blessings upon him – begat from a Coptic woman.' Then he pulled her up by the arm onto his horse and rode off with her. The girl's father, bent and filthy, ran after them brandishing a lump of the fecund mud in his hands. 'With God's blessings,' he murmured, after the Sheikh placed a coin of pure gold in his astonished palm.

She undid the dirty belt from her waist so that he could look upon the body that was like a piece of smooth white cheese. The body, rounded like a morsel of moist halva, surrendered to his touch. The grandmother – whose name would soon become 'the Guest' – bathed for the first time in a basin of pure copper and combed out the long, luxuriant hair that Hend would inherit. The fish tattoos flexed and gleamed in the water that streamed over her body and the servants sang to her from the other side of the door.

> *Whose daughter is this in the village,*
> *you whose shawl has been caught?*
> *I'm betrothed to the Chief of Arabs,*
> *he whose uncle is a prince.*

The Chief of Bedouins disliked houses because of their low, cramped roofs. He lived in a large tent pitched in the middle of an open expanse of land. His wives lived in the compound in a series of adjoining mud-brick rooms that opened onto the sandy court-yard. On the other side stood a similar row of rooms, the kitchens and granaries. A group of palm trees stood between the two rows. The Guest was not given one of these rooms in the main com-pound. She was like a frightened she-camel and it would take her some time to settle down. The grandfather built two rooms for her alone up on one of the smaller elevations of Pharaoh's Hills. She never visited the women down below and not once did she cross the perimeters of the main compound. She never witnessed the hustle and bustle of the kitchens nor smelled the pungent odours of milling day. She would hear the noise and guess at what was happening in the granaries. From a distance she would watch the shadows of the women running back and forth between the rooms. The Guest would sit in front of her house and wait for the young servant girls, pungent with kitchen odours, to come to her. They would step inside quickly and set her meal down with a perfunctory greeting, then run back outside without giving her a chance to exchange a single word. They never called her 'Mistress' or 'Auntie', only 'the Guest' or 'the master's foreign woman', names that were a summing up of her place in the world.

Her husband brought her precious gifts of Damascene silk and fine cotton cloth from Ashmun. Whenever loneliness crept upon her, she would run her hand over one of her black velvet gowns and, taking up the needle, begin to embroider its bodice with sequins and little bits of coloured glass. A rope on which she hung these gowns stretched along the length of the wall of her room. As time passed, the gowns piled up on the rope and it sagged like her breasts, from the burden of the heavy weight.

She would perfume her gowns with incense and musk and lay them out in the eye of the noonday sun – to preserve them from moth eggs, or perhaps to provoke the envy of her co-wives. At night she would stuff their pockets with henna and basil leaves and stow them away under the mattresses to smooth out the creases. Then she would sit and keep watch on the gates of the high encircling wall from the corner of her eye.

The Guest was not inclined to conversation. On the rare occasions when she did speak, she would tell the same story about the husband who owned a caravan of camels laden with wooden chests that travelled between Gaza and Khan Yunis. The chests were piled high with grain and they came back with olive oil and bars of Aleppo soap, robes of silk and Meccan velvet and Yemeni incense. The wives of this husband were many, she said, but it was she alone who mothered a male child.

'As soon as I emptied my belly of an infant,' she said, 'I'd put him in the basket and send him to the big tent for his father to hold. The child would come back silent and listless every time, and after a night or two, his face would puff up and turn blue and then he would die. When the fifth boy-child came, I said to myself, "The evil eye can shatter rock." I piled rags over the basket and said to the women, "The boy has died. He's followed his brothers." Then I placed him on my breast and he nursed, sleepy and soft like a ball of white cotton. Our Lady Mary came to me in my sleep and took him from my breast and plunged him in holy water and in the morning he was pink and white like a rose. The Saviour and the Virgin decreed that he should live when I feared he would go to the place the others had gone. Then I sent him to his father and he said, "God be praised," and named him Ibrahim.'

The Guest loved to exercise her nimble fingers. She loved to winnow cotton, peel garlic, and strip corncobs of their brittle husks. She twisted rope out of fibre and the wicks of kerosene lamps out of cotton and she wove mats out of strips of bamboo. If she had nothing else to weave, she would twist thin paper cones out of bits of old newspapers; these she used to light the kerosene lamps in order to save matches. On that hill opposite the tent of the Bedouin Chief, she would weave and sing and see after her hens. From time to time she would dip her feet into the running waters of the canal. She was a peasant and could not live without soil and animals.

Little Hend would fall asleep in the Guest's lap as she flung open the gates to her world of marvellous stories. She always began these stories in the same way. 'If our house were close by . . .' she would whisper, 'if our house were close by . . .' And yet she had no other house. Her house was their house. Hend would squat next to her as she emptied the cotton stuffing from the pillowcases onto the floor and spread it out in the sun, pulling it to make it light and fluffy like spun sugar. In the grandmother's stories, the maidens endlessly laboured over the recalcitrant cotton, pulling and teasing it for the velvety smooth pillows that would receive the sweat of love and childbirth, and the tears of desertion and loss. The pillows that cradle our sleeping faces and catch our dreams at night should be soft and secret. Hend lay her head in the Guest's lap and listened as she began to tell a story: 'If my father's house were close by—'

'Where is your father's house?' the girl interrupted her. The Guest laughed as she tried to remember. 'Near the village threshing ground? Past the Valley of the Angel? Behind the salt marshes on the White Estate?' (The grandmother did not know that the White Estate on which she lived was now called the Mosque Estate.) She said, trying to pinpoint the very moment: 'One day your grandfather, may he rest in peace, passed our way. I was standing there at the door of the house . . . sweeping the floor? No! I was picking cotton in the fields of the Bedouin tribes . . .' She went on to tell the story of how he came and took her away on his horse and shut her up in a house with high walls. The Guest gazed at the open sky but she couldn't tell east from west, and she didn't know whether any member of her family was still alive. She still dreamt of walking along the bank of that faraway canal, of scrubbing her dress in the running water, and scraping the heels of her feet on a sieve at the top of a field planted with broad beans. She strung broad beans together in necklaces that Hend wore around her neck. Hend hopped around her grandmother like a rabbit and scurried off to run her errands. The Guest sent her from time to time to buy a few candles from Salim the druggist's shop. When Hend returned, she plied her with questions about a long-ago world.

'Is Salim still alive?'

Hend nodded her head.

'Does he still run the shop?'

Hend shook her head.

'Who's at the counter?'

Hend moved her lips lazily to form a brief answer. 'His son.'

'Is Abu Ma'tuq's house still opposite Salim's shop?'

Hend didn't know who Abu Ma'tuq was. She didn't recognise half the names that the Guest remembered, but she nodded her head to assure her that everything was still just as it was in her imagination. The threshing machine still stood on the edge of the Bedouin field opposite the Muqawi Aqueduct and the migrant labourers still lived in the salt marshes. All those folk who peopled her memory – shop owners, carpenters, fishmongers – were still there, as she remembered them to be long ago.

Hend had no idea why they called her grandmother the Guest, nor why her clothes were stowed away in a wooden chest as though she were forever on the verge of embarking on some voyage or other, or why she took out her velvet gown at the beginning of each

42

season, perfumed it, then carefully refolded it and placed it back in the chest. Hend was mesmerised by the dark freckles stamped on her face, the same ones she had inherited along with her long hair, her short stature, and her dark and brooding disposition.

She herself is still that same restless child, she muses, always looking for a suitcase in which to pile clothes grown tired of being shut up in closets, a travelling case that she can place under her pillow for safe keeping, a thing to be seized and whisked away in anger, a thing to rest her head upon in sorrow. In her dreams she sees the Guest passing her fingers over her palm and stroking the lifeline there. She laughs and says, 'The way of Abu Zayd the Wanderer.' Hend did not know then that her life would become a smouldering fire, a long exile, like that of the legendary Abu Zayd. Her restless spirit was no longer content with stories of fleet camels and noble steeds and fiery comets shooting through the corridors of the sky. The journey of winter and summer in those stories was not enough to plug the pit of fear in her heart. Hend slept in the Guest's lap whenever she grew tired of the coarse, cruel pillows that refused to give up their tenderness. In the dream she would say to her:

> If my father's house were close by
> I'd go and bring a plate of raisins
> for you to eat and then you'd pray over the beloved
> for all lovers pray to God to pray for the beloved.

Sleep would overcome her and the dreams that followed would carry her across the seven seas.

Then the dreams came true at a single stroke. Here she is now, walking down Flatbush Avenue without a map. She has come to know a good number of streets by heart. She spends her days sitting in front of the huge discount supermarket in which she often shops. She examines the store circular and compares. She's learned the essential words by now, words like 'savings' and 'coupons' and 'buy one get one free'. She walks through Greenwood Cemetery and examines the crosses on the tombstones and tries to forget the grandmother who lived in a small house on top of the hill and never once left it.

The grandmother died hugging her wooden cross to her chest and was buried in the family crypt with the following epitaph: 'The Guest, mother of children, God rest her soul and lead her into His vast gardens of Paradise.' She left nothing behind but a small wooden chest in which she had packed her many dresses of satin and velvet embroidered with fishes and dolls, and a short rope on which had hung a gown of black velvet, fragrant and still, never once soiled by the dusty ground. In a smaller cardboard box she left a few candles and needles and bits of soap, while in the nooks and crannies of the room she had carefully placed a few stray strands of the hair that had fallen out over the years from pregnancy and childbirth, the death of suckling babes, and the endless days, both white and black.

4

South Slope

Long ago, before Fourth Avenue became Fourth Avenue, the entire area was made up of Dutch farms spreading out over the fertile slope of eastern Brooklyn. The Saturday market is the last remaining trace of that distant world. It is a vegetable and poultry market, mostly frequented by artists shopping for natural or 'organic' foods and enchanted by the din and the air of nostalgia that hovers about the place. Hend likes the Fourth Avenue market because the prices are reasonable and she can bargain there. She likes to sit on the sidewalk of the wide avenue on Saturdays and watch the young women in the stiff brown wigs that hide their shaved heads going in and out of the Jewish synagogues nearby.

She stares at their long black skirts and heavy coats curiously. They nod their heads shyly at her and sometimes they stop to ask if she is Jewish. She quickly shakes her head in the negative before they have a chance to hand her one of their fliers: printed invitations to visit the House of God. She prefers to steer clear of those kind of invitations. The sidewalk of Fourth Avenue is wide like a terrace and it hosts a second-hand market that they call a *flea market* in English. Things no longer wanted by their owners are piled up on the pavement for sale: kitchen utensils, old clothes and shoes, wooden boxes, framed paintings, photo albums whose owners are long dead, records with pictures of Elvis Presley, Liza

Minnelli, or Frank Sinatra on the sleeve, antique cameras, entire libraries spilling out of their cartons, notebooks still carrying the imprint of their owners' fingers. The most intimate moments of ordinary people transformed into stacks of abandoned memories, legacies to be picked over by cheerful amateur collectors once the bones of their former keepers have finally been deposited in Greenwood Cemetery. Hend likes to sit with her friend Emilia as she spreads out her wares on the pavement. Emilia knows all the styles and brand names of her old shoes by heart, and she prices them according to decade of origin: 1950s, 1960s, and 1970s. 'They call this stuff "vintage",' she tells Hend. 'I don't know why Americans are so crazy about it. Maybe it comes in handy for Halloween parties and such. All the young actor-types around town know me. They come all the way from Manhattan: "Hey, Emilia, I need a pair of Marilyn Monroe shoes." Those crazy kids are always looking for outlandish things.'

Hend passes through the South Slope district daily because her son's school is nearby. She likes the wide streets and the way the meagre winter sun passes slowly across the sky above. She likes to watch the old women sitting out in the sun like her and trying to recollect the years that had vanished so quickly. She likes to sit on the wooden bench and watch Jojo tell fortunes from across the street. Emilia sits next to her and smiles. Her grey coat looks exactly like the one Hend is wearing. She's short and thin, with a slight stoop. Her face is covered in fine wrinkles and tufts of white hair sprout from unexpected places, like her nostrils and the edges of her upper lip. Her eyes are sharp and alert. They look like two balls of fire, and when she opens her mouth wide to laugh she exposes a row of stained, broken teeth. She pulls her coat up around her when she sits down and takes off her shoes and socks to sun her feet. She moves her bare, swollen legs back and forth as though she were a child on a swing, and the downy hair that covers them gleams in the sunlight. Emilia likes to talk a lot, and when she gets started on the story of her long life it's almost impossible to interrupt her. She keeps mysterious coupons in a cloth purse and organises them carefully so that she can find exactly what she wants when she needs it. She talks with great authority about how to save pennies and where to find the cheapest stuff but she also loves to philosophise about life.

Hend met her for the first time at the library, at a talk about how the media shapes public opinion in the United States. Emilia was sitting in the front row because she was hard of hearing. She had simply removed the 'reserved' sign on the chair and sat down. Hend was sitting right behind her and, before the event had even gotten under way, Emilia started talking to anyone who would listen about the meaning of critical thinking. She said that she was a citizen of the former Soviet Union and that she had emigrated to America with her husband in the 1970s during the Cold War. Her husband – who had retired long ago – used to be a physics professor and he had come to the States as a political refugee. She talked about how she had lived her whole life in a country with an official state media, but that after twenty years of living in New York (she was now almost eighty years old) she had grown even more tired of the supposedly 'free' media here. It reminded her of the old Soviet days, the propaganda, the calculated manipulation of people's tastes, thoughts, and choices. Now the only thing she watched was Dr Phil, and sometimes Oprah, while her husband preferred to watch the BBC. She had come to America without knowing a single word of English. She and her husband had moved into a mixed Russian and Latino neighbourhood, and she could have easily spent the rest of her life without learning any English at all. But she liked to listen to the tiny transistor radio that she took everywhere with her, and that's how she learned to speak the language.

Emilia talked on and on without pausing once. The panellists looked at each other in dismay and wondered who was going to be the one to gently put an end to her homily on American television and radio. No one dared. She was a forceful speaker, and always on high alert against any attempt to shut her down. People in the audience began to drift off, one after the other, some quietly, others muttering angrily, until no one was left except for Hend, who remained sitting right behind her, waiting. That was the beginning of their friendship. Emilia's easy, undemanding companionship was soothing to Hend, and Emilia grew attached to Hend because she listened to her quietly till the very end, and went along with her to book discussions and lectures. Emilia always came up with clippings and fliers advertising upcoming events of that kind, and she meticulously noted dates and times and venues in a little notebook that she kept for the purpose. She often called Hend to invite her to this or that event. The two women enjoyed each other's company.

Emilia's husband hated going out. He liked to cook and do the housework as he listened to his favourite classical music. He worshipped peace and quiet and so he never gave Emilia the chance to open her mouth.

Emilia waits for Hend every morning on the wooden bench in front of the green market on Fourth Avenue. Together they soak up the thin sunlight and drink coffee out of paper cups. They watch the passers-by and exchange food coupons and news about free events or classes: dancing and cooking classes; street fairs and cultural festivals: the Middle Eastern Festival, the Brooklyn Jazz Festival, book signings at the library, and so on.

They sit together in silence, like carbon copies perched on a paradoxical wooden bench. They gaze out at the stingy winter sun. Emilia begins to lay out the coupons that she doesn't really need. She gives Hend the ones for diapers and baby food. Then, as though suddenly remembering something, she asks her, 'How old is your son?'

'Eight,' Hend replies.

Emilia takes the coupons back from Hend and puts them in her purse. 'Okay. Take this instead.' But Hend refuses.

'You're still young, you can use this stuff.'

Hend shakes her head again. 'I don't need them any more.'

'You're still young. It's only temporary.'

'It stopped years ago.'

Emilia nods her head sympathetically. 'I got menopause when I came to this country. I was still young back then . . . fifty-seven years old.'

Hend just nods her head and doesn't say anything. Emilia gets up all of a sudden and crosses the street to her Mexican friend Jojo's storefront. Jojo is Abd al-Karim's ex-wife, and she tells fortunes now. A sign hangs in the glass window: *Your fortune told. Palm readings, zodiac, tarot.*

Hend sits there on the bench by herself, clutching coupons for sanitary napkins that she doesn't need. Her eyes fall on the spider web of thin varicose veins that has sprouted on her leg. She slowly tears up the coupons into small pieces and drops them into the empty coffee cup.

Emilia comes and goes, for no particular reason, without hellos or goodbyes. Now she comes back and sits next to her again, picking up the threads of a conversation that she alone can begin and end. She smells like all old people: an obscure, undefinable smell that time deposits without making any excuses. Hend knows that smell well from her childhood days, when she used to trail around after an old woman who worked in her father's house. People used to call her Grandmother Zaynab from before anyone could remember. Grandmother Zaynab was chocolate brown but when she stood in front of the clay oven in the courtyard her skin took on the colour of dry crusty bread. She would spill a pail of washing water over her bare neck and chest, which were burning hot from the stinging flames of the oven, then wet an old rag in the pail to wipe down the oven rack. A small woman squatted behind her to help her with the baking. As soon as Grandmother Zaynab eased a loaf into the mouth of the oven, she would say, 'Hand me another one, sister,' and the woman would scoop out a round lump of dough in the palm of her hand and place it on the bread paddle. The balls of dough were magically transformed into perfectly formed loaves of bread as they came out of the oven's mouth.

Grandmother Zaynab was not her grandmother. She was no relative at all. Her voice rang with that Delta accent that distinguished the outsiders from the Bedouin. Her official job was to bake the family's weekly bread but she would also come to prepare for the dough-making ritual. She washed the wheat and spread it out on bamboo mats, scented it with grains of fenugreek and lupine and rough corn, and carried it on her head to the distant mill. She kept the keys to the grain storerooms, scrubbed the kneading basins, and collected the dry tree leaves to fuel the oven. Every Friday she came to sprinkle the corners of the house with blessed herbs and water and salt, murmuring invocations against the evil eye of the enviers: *there is no might or grace save in God*. She gave the people of the house enchanted water to drink to chase away mischievous spirits and prepared steaming earthenware pots of pigeons and rice on feast days like Ashura and Ragabiya and the first of Sha'ban. People said that her hand was blessed. She would dip it in olive oil and rub her mother's constantly aching back, or set the sprains and fractures of the boys who were always tripping and falling and breaking bones from bouncing off the walls. Grandmother Zaynab was not their servant. There was nothing about her that suggested this. She worked in other houses besides theirs, delivering babies and tying the umbilical cords of newborns, treating aches and pains with ointments made from camphor and linseed oil and applying plaster with an agile and practised hand. Her forehead boasted a green tattoo in the form of a fish. Another plastic fish hung from a cord around her neck and the same green fishes also decorated her wrist. Her nostrils were split from the weight of a ring that had once ornamented her nose and left behind a sharp vertical slash.

Grandmother Zaynab's hair was like white cotton candy. She

used to rub the parting with soft butter to make it shine. She moved through the house like a length of thin, dry, hollowed-out sugar-cane, a heavy anklet of pure silver clasped around one skinny leg. She lived in a mud hut that had been built against the wall of the baking rooms. Hend used to climb the low wall straight into the heart of Grandmother Zaynab's house. 'Grandmother, Mama wants you.' A little while later, Grandmother Zaynab would come to the house to milk the cows and make the cheese and collect the eggs and check up on the duck sitting on her chicks. She packed the coals into the water pipe and the thick smoke crept out of her split nose as she laughed. 'The pipe chases away the ghouls in your head.'

Grandmother Zaynab regularly attended Sheikha Safina's weekly exorcism. She put on her green gown on Thursday market day and wrapped her head in a white scarf. She came back from the market and laid her bundles down on the ground. 'I'm going to the dakka,' she would curtly inform them. 'I'll see you later.' She disappeared from high noon to sunset and always came back exhausted and speechless. She would lay her body down in the western balcony and passers-by would hear her talking sleepily to her invisible qarina.

When Hend went into the baking room that day, all she wanted was to watch the soft, hot bread coming out of the burning mouth of the oven. 'Give me a little one, Grandmother,' she murmured, mesmerised by the movement of the bread paddle sliding the soft dough into the oven. A 'little one' was a miniature loaf of bread made especially for children. Grandmother Zaynab, who was busy finishing her story, ignored the girl. '. . . And I said, by God, don't you dare raise your hand against me!' Hend knew that Grandmother Zaynab was telling the story of her first husband to her qarina. She had heard the story many times before: 'He started hitting me on my face and saying, "Where were you, you bitch?" and me saying to him, "I had to fulfil my vow to Sheikha Safina." He didn't let go of me until he had knocked out this big tooth,' and she opened her mouth to show her qarina the big gap there. Hend repeated herself irritably, 'I want a little one *now*, Grandmother.' But the Grandmother was busy talking and wiping down the top of the oven. 'He left me lying there just like this old rag, sister.' She pointed to the ash rag, then added, 'He went to do his ablutions at the canal bridge and he started invoking the Prophet's name, but he'd forgotten that the switchblade he'd just slashed me with was still in his pocket. It was sharp!' and she pointed to a jagged scar on her face. 'I warned him, "God's command! God's prohibition!" But he had no faith in God or man. The switchblade cut into his stomach as he was washing himself for prayer and he was already done for by the time they brought him home to me.'

Hend was bored of listening by now, and angry at Grandmother Zaynab for ignoring her. 'Come on, Grandmother!' she shouted impatiently.

Grandmother's face grew red like a burning coal and she picked up a piece of firewood and waved it furiously at her, 'Get out of here, girl! No little ones for you.'

They were used to her sudden inexplicable fits of anger. She would shoo away the children like a barren bitch, then a few minutes later turn and pat their heads with her rough hand, dip the small loaf in molasses and feed the open mouths around her in a gentle token of peace. Hend wasn't afraid of her, though. She scooped up a handful of dirt from the ground and threw it in her face. The second time she did it, the dirt settled on the soft balls of dough. She ran off and didn't stop running until she got to the flame tree and scurried up it breathlessly. Grandmother Zaynab ran after her, brandishing a long stout stick and shouting threats. When Hend finally came down, the rough hand seized her, dragged her into the dark room, and shut the old wooden door fast. Half the day went by with her locked up behind that door. The damp mud room was full of hidden rabbit lairs and piles of green clover. The rabbits hopped around surreptitiously in the clover, suddenly emerging into the open with twitching jaws, then scurrying back, trembling, into their holes. Hend sat there on the black basalt stone behind the door and stared at the dark holes as the skylights above sifted the meagre light coming in from the washed-out crimson sky.

Grandmother Zaynab eventually came back carrying the miniature loaf of bread and some honey, but the girl, who had wet herself, didn't open her mouth. She made her drink some enchanted water from the fright pan, and then she made her jump seven times over a bowl of burning Javanese incense, but it didn't do any good. Hend grew listless and her eyes took on a strange, faraway look. A few days later she claimed that she had seen Grandmother Zaynab in the shape of a green toad the colour of clover hopping around on the pile of vegetable scraps, and that she had stuck out her white lizard tongue at Hend and ordered her to lick her belly and then swallow the saliva afterwards. Hend was afraid of the dark and of the scurrying rabbits, so she did it.

She licked the green toad's belly and then she wet herself. She kept on wetting herself for many years after that and the pungent, acrid smell of urine clung to her clothes no matter what she did.

Grandmother Zaynab stayed at their house for weeks after this incident. She sprinkled blessed herbs throughout the house and chanted magical incantations. She washed the girl's body in rose water and clothed her in a spotless white dress and took her to see Sheikha Safina. She lit seven candles in the Sheikha's window and said, 'By your darling prophet don't fail me now. I'm the one who scared the wits out of the girl.' But Hend kept wetting herself. In her dreams, the green toad pursued her down secret subterranean passages, foamy spittle leaking from its mouth.

One evening Grandmother Zaynab ruffled Hend's hair and yawned as she started to tell her stories about long-ago travellers. Her sharp eyes picked out a few grey hairs that had begun to sprout on the girl's head – a girl who was not yet ten – and she noticed that the roots had begun to turn white too. So she put the henna to soak in boiled tea with black seed, then applied it to Hend's long hair, transforming it into a curtain of deep black and flaming red. The white embers cleaved the roots and sprouted again. Grandmother Zaynab sighed in despair and said, 'I don't know what to do with this daughter of yours, mistress.' Her mother added three new nicknames for Hend to her list: 'Little demon', 'Loopy', and 'Head-in-the-clouds'.

✼

Hend and Emilia stroll up and down the wide sidewalks of Fourth Avenue so that Emilia can inspect cartons full of bric-a-brac that their owners have thrown away: books and pictures, anything that has become old and useless and disposable. Hend reads the phrase *take me if you want* printed in Magic Marker on the sides of the cartons. She wonders at this oblique expression, and she feels that it is somehow directed at her.

Emilia rummages in the cartons for old shoes and empty bottles. She pokes around slowly and patiently in garbage cans. On Saturdays, she takes her choicest treasures to the flea market and spreads them out next to the other vendors. Emilia specialises in shoes. 'Marilyn Monroe shoes,' she calls out to passers-by. 'I've got Audrey Hepburn, Farrah Fawcett . . . I've got kids' shoes too.'

Hend tells Emilia that she reminds her of so many people she's met in her life. Emilia laughs, revealing the gaps in her mouth where teeth used to be. 'I know, I know. Everybody says that I look like the old woman in *Zorba the Greek*. It's too bad I never saw that movie. I don't know about Mrs Zorba, but all old people look alike, my dear.'

Scattered raindrops fall on Emilia's frail, wrinkled face. Hend leaves her to her never-ending task of poking through abandoned cardboard boxes. She goes to sit on the wooden bench in front of her son's school while her eyes follow Emilia as she moves further and further away, pushing the little cart piled high with shoes that fit her and others that don't.

5

Coco Bar

The smell of fresh beer wafts up from old wooden barrels in the little bar right under her window. She likes the smell of beer because it reminds her of her father. Grandmother Zaynab used to say, 'Your father was popular with the ladies, God rest his soul. He used to walk around the Heights and the girls would sing to him from behind their windows.' Fatma al-Qarumiya used to compose poetry about him:

> *He's the lovely one who passed beneath our window*
> *Beneath our window his lips drip honey*
> *Beneath our window, and what can I do, girls?*
> *Beneath our window, he's the lovely one who passed through.*

He was handsome and refined, and he always wore elegant suits. That's what Hend still remembers about her father. It was a lot of extra work for her mother. She ironed his white pocket handkerchiefs, folded and organised his socks, and carefully matched his neckties. Another photo in the family album: her father stands in front of the auditorium of the Faculty of Law at King Fuad University, looking trim and smart. For some reason that Hend doesn't fully understand, he never took a job after graduation. He hung a sign that said 'Lawyer for Misdemeanours in the Civil

Courts' on the door of the reception house on the hill, but he didn't have an office or clients, and he never attended court proceedings except when he wanted to see his friends. Every day he left the house in his elegant suit, his jacket unbuttoned, his black hair slicked back with Vaseline, and strolled down the alleys, where he was known as a distinguished man of leisure. He religiously attended all the agricultural cooperative meetings, the municipal assembly meetings, and the local council meetings. All these organisations were housed in the same red-brick building in the centre of the town and her father's educated friends were all to be found there: Doctor Shamil the pharmacist, Mr Emile the school principal, and His Excellency the President of the Municipal Assembly, whoever he happened to be at the time.

These were the same men who would regularly meet in the evenings in her father's cosy reception house. It was a small house perched high above Pharaoh's Hills where a woman called the Guest used to live. Hend would constantly find excuses to go there. She would climb up the hill bringing him anything he might need: 'Father, do you want dinner? Father, do you want fresh clothes? Father, do you want some snacks?' Her mother prepared small trays of home-made pickles and boiled broad beans marinated in lemon juice, and Hend carried them up to the reception house. Sometimes her mother sent her to ask for money. Hend hated carrying that particular message. Her brothers simply refused to do it. The daily negotiation over money was always conducted through her. Sometimes her father would explode into a barrage of curses that she knew by heart: 'Money, money, money! Do you think I'm sitting on a money machine?

Minting shitty new coins every day?' But faced with Hend's un-flinching, reproachful gaze, he would finally give in and hand her a few silver coins from his pocket. Sometimes Hend would go back empty-handed, with only the curt message: 'I don't have any.' Her mother's nose would colour slightly, then she would sigh heavily after listening to Hend repeat those four words that seemed to encapsulate the entire story of her misfortunes, and Hend knew that this sigh was the harbinger of a breakdown that was sure to envelop the whole house in a flood of misery and gloom.

Sometimes she went up to the reception house for no particu-lar reason. 'Mama says go see if your father wants anything' was the innocent phrase she used as a password. Only she was allowed to play this little trick. Her father always had a smile for his little girl. He could never manage to be harsh with her, even if he tried.

After the death of the Guest, her father hung his sign on the door to remind everyone that he was still officially a lawyer at the Higher Court of Appeals. In point of fact, he believed that the courts were a waste of time, and that reception houses like his were the proper place to solve disputes. He spent every even-ing up there with his friends. Hend would sometimes hear Fatma al-Qarumiya's voice coming from inside and the ring of her long voluptuous laugh mingling with the laughter of the men, but on those occasions she never dared to disturb them.

At school, everyone respected Hend because her father always made a point of attending the parents' meetings that no one else ever went to. The first time he went, he sat with the school principal, Mr Emile, and they chatted about things like the im-portance of raising the town's abysmal educational standards. Her father gave Mr Emile one of his Dunhill Red cigarettes and the man practically fainted with joy as he accepted the proffered offering and launched into his favourite subject. 'Your Excellency, I've got more than one hundred students in my school and the municipality doesn't give us a single penny, not even to fix the school bell. Imagine, Your Excellency, I have to use this whistle to signal the start of classes!' Her father knew that Mr Emile spent most of his spare time sitting in front of the small bicycle-repair shop (which also doubled as a warehouse) that he had recently opened next to the school courtyard, but the principal quickly became a bosom friend of her father's. Hend would watch him busily preparing plates of hot sausage in the reception house and setting out cold bottles of beer as he laughed out loud at some joke or other. The sound struck Hend as strange, because Mr Emile rarely laughed. From time to time he would declare, 'By God, Your Excellency, you've made our stay in this godforsaken place easier to bear. The village would have been terribly lonely without these little soirées of yours.'

Hend knows that her father made life a lot more pleasant for outsiders like Mr Emile and Doctor Shamil, as well as the women who came to the village from other parts of the country. The reception house became a temporary home for some of them: Miss Ibtisam, for example, the music teacher from Port Said who wore provocatively short skirts, and Miss Fayqa, the home economics teacher who taught her mother how to crochet the duck stitch. The reception house up on the hill hosted many a lady teacher for a few weeks at a time. Hend would take them their breakfast tray in the morning and their dinner tray in the evening, and at the end of their appointed stay some of them would come down to the house to thank her mother for her hospitality. They would sit with her for a little while in the western balcony and teach her how to crochet a new stitch or how to use hair curlers and dress a chignon. Some of them didn't come at all, though. Some contrived to make husbands of the village's petty bureaucrats, while others left town pretty quickly because Pharaoh's Hills 'is a tiny, bone-dry, backward village', or so they said. The nurses who worked at the local hospital were also habitués of the reception house, and these women almost never went down to the main house to greet her mother. It was Doctor Shamil who introduced the new girls to their evening soirées, and he ended up marrying more than one of them. Most of them simply left as suddenly as they had arrived, leaving Fatma al-Qarumiya to laugh out loud in her opaque, masculine voice – the undisputed queen of the circle of men.

Her father's generosity was not limited to hosting itinerant female guests. He also liked to resolve ongoing disputes between the local families. His powers of persuasion were superlative, what with his aristocratic looks, his clean, elegant suits, and his deep, melodious voice. Besides, the courts' tentacles were long and tangled and people preferred to avoid them if they could. The preparations for these reconciliation sessions were elaborate. Clean rush mats were spread out on the floor of the reception house, pots of tea and coffee were served, and sometimes, if a satisfactory settlement was reached amongst the parties, small animals were slaughtered and roasted over an open fire. Her father, dressed in his beautiful Bedouin cloak, would lean back comfortably on the mat against a pile of pillows and reel off the relevant provisions of the criminal code, the sayings of Imam Ali, and the counsel of the prophets, and back up his claims with ringing Quranic verses. The feuding clans were almost invariably persuaded to accept judgment of a few kilos of grain, five Egyptian pounds, or occasionally an inch of land separating their respective waterwheels, because 'possession belongs to God alone'. After the warm welcome, the tea and coffee, and the elaborate feasting, the feuding parties would leave the reception house content, and for the next few weeks her father would be easy and cheerful.

Her mother in her honey-coloured robe would say to him in a disapproving tone that he pretended not to understand: 'Why do you always have to wear yourself out for other people?' He would shake his head wearily and reply, 'You're the daughter of Bedouin Arabs. You of all people should understand our customs. You know it's a duty.' Whenever he called her 'cousin', her mother would smile one of her rare smiles because it meant that he was pleased with her; that he would sleep in his own bed for the next few days and that he'd narrate the story of the feud to her over and over and in great detail, carefully explaining exactly how he artfully managed to put an end to the crisis. However, if she crossed the red line, if she complained or criticised too much, if she dared to say (in that angry, resentful voice of hers that he knew so well), 'What have we got to do with all these problems? Banquets and parties and expenses every other day! My children come first and your own household is more important,' the peaceful conversation would turn into a violent argument. He'd storm out angrily through the eastern door, shouting bitter remarks about grief and worry and tiresome women. He'd slam the glass door a couple of times and spend the night in the reception house high above Pharaoh's Hills. He'd light the brazier and the air would become thick with the smell of incense and hashish and cigarette smoke and melancholy – not to mention Fatma al-Qarumiya's heavy perfume. Fatma's deep laugh would set her plump white flesh shaking merrily: 'I've told you time and again, cousin, living with women is a miserable state of affairs.'

✲

Her father liked to read. He read a lot because he wanted to seem like an expert on everything. He read biographies of Christopher Columbus and Edward Lane. He read about places he'd never seen before, like the lands of the White Nile and Mount Lebanon. He talked about Paris and Naples and Tangiers and he gave his friends in the reception house the impression that he was a seasoned traveller. They acted as though they believed him when he spoke confidently and bolstered his words with convincing details. Hend did believe him. She rode the sea of his imagination and saw ships and distant harbours there. His friends pretended to believe him for the sake of the party and the sheer delight of make-believe. Doctor Shamil told them all stories about how he had travelled to important conferences and invented new drugs for epilepsy and bed sores and arthritis. He was an expert at mixing up a special hashish-and-opium paste that he claimed could vanquish every disease but prostate cancer, for which, God preserve us, there was no cure. They would all laugh because they knew that the important conferences he went to were just a few dozen kilometres away in Alexandria, and that they were more often than not nothing but fishing expeditions for fair-skinned prostitutes. They also knew that he was hopelessly addicted to the opium that whittled away at his brain. Mr Emile liked to tell extravagant stories about his virility. He was short, thin, dark-skinned, and very hairy. The macho fantasies that he wove around his scrawny body were truly comic but everyone got a kick out of his risqué jokes because they went well with the sausages and cucumbers and pickles. Fatma al-Qarumiya, meanwhile, claimed that her ancestry went back to the Prophet's illustrious line at Mecca and that she was purer even than the folk heroine al-Khadra al-Sharifa. She was both a mother and a whore and the womanly smoke she blew out from her water pipe stirred up the men's admiration and provoked their lust.

Her father was in the habit of drinking a beer or two before he went to bed every night. She would run over to Amm Mahmud's shop and say, 'Two bottles of Stella beer and a pack of Dunhill cigarettes, please.' He had been sleeping in the reception house for days. Smoke drifted out from behind the door as Hend approached. 'Mama told me to come and ask if you want anything.' They walked side by side, hands clasped. They passed the threshing machine and the Muqawi Aqueduct and a string of small mud houses. He pointed to things as they walked by. 'That was your Grandfather Sulayman's estate, and this was your late Grandmother Shaqawa's guest house, and this is the Raml Aqueduct.' She stumbled on the stones scattered in the sand as she walked next to him. On the way back home, tired and worn out, he smiled sadly. He stretched out on the balcony and the children formed a circle around him.

He began to tell the story of the Prophet Moses. 'Pray for the Prophet,' he said between each part, but Hend preferred the tale of the Prophet Joseph. She liked the sound of her father's sad voice as he told it in between mouthfuls of yellow foamy beer. 'Son, tell not thy vision to thy brothers lest they lay a trap for thee, for Satan is a mortal enemy of man.' He liked to repeat that particular verse. He knew the Quranic text by heart and never made a mistake in pronunciation or punctuation. He slowly sipped at his beer as he talked. 'He said, "My son, enter not from the same door, rather enter from different doors."' Her mother would sometimes interrupt to point out the dangers of the envier's evil eye. His head would be in her lap at this point, and her fingers would be playing with his hair while the children sat around his feet, small, wide-eyed, and hanging on to every word formed by that deep voice that drew them all like a magnet. As she listened, Hend dreamt of becoming a great prophet or saint, carrying a large rod with which to cleave the sea or running through the desert, plumes of water spurting up from beneath her feet. She was always fantasising about being a character in an epic, and her Arabic teacher encouraged these fantasies: 'You'll do great things one day, inshallah.'

She began to seek out a real-world instrument for her greatness to manifest itself and found it in Angele, an easy victim. Angele was round and plump, like a short, dark bear, and she always sat at the back of the classroom, quiet and timid. Her features seemed to have been moulded from a mixture of mud and sweat and they were stamped with an expression of astonishing simplicity. Hend began her self-appointed mission of guiding humanity with

Angele. She would take her aside and talk to her about how she absolutely had to repeat the phrase 'There is no God but God' so that she could enter the gates of Paradise as a good Muslim. Angele would shake her head miserably but Hend kept insisting. 'Just say it in your head – the important thing is to go to Paradise.' Angele took out a piece of soft bread filled with halva from her dirty cloth bag and held out half of it to Hend. 'Want a piece of my sandwich?' That was how she always tried to change the subject and safely evade the iron grip of her would-be saviour.

Angele was always lurking next to walls because she was afraid of running around and bumping into people. Her step was hesitant and slow; she was always kind to others but sometimes she acted terribly stupid. She didn't understand the jibes the other girls flung at her. She was resigned to it all – she was incapable of being any other way – and this dull indifference saved her a lot of trouble. She listened to all Hend's attempts to convert her without comment or resentment. She would just nod her head gently and say, 'Only God can show us the way.' She repeated this phrase as though it were a cheerful incantation; as though she truly believed that there might be some hope in this promised awakening to God's will after all. But Hend didn't give up on her chosen disciple until she disappeared from school altogether one day. Only then did she accept that she had definitively lost her first great battle in the war to deliver humanity from error.

Hend was the first girl at school to put on the long, flowing hijab. This was also part of her mission to transform herself into a storybook heroine. The other girls – even the peasant girls – wore light scarves on their heads that left their long, thick braids uncovered. Hend wrapped a thick, heavy scarf over her entire head. 'God commanded women to wear the khimar, not a transparent scrap of cloth,' she would proclaim in order to show off her piety and asceticism. She began to turn her eyes away from the sight of her father's evening bottle of beer and she often begged God to forgive him. Soon, many of the other girls followed her example and started wearing the heavy khimar to show that they were just as pious and modest. Not to be outdone in the fear of God, Hend went one step further and started wearing dark, forbidding colours: black or navy blue. She even took to wearing a pair of black gloves in public. ('I don't shake hands with men – may God curse those who do.') She trod a long road of self-abnegation and self-praise and she clung to it tenaciously, even after she had read the Quranic commentaries and discovered that the prohibition in question actually referred to bodies coming together in the act of love, and that it had nothing to do with a simple handshake. Nonetheless, she continued to insist that men and women were prohibited from shaking hands in Islam and that the act opened the door to lustful thoughts and actions. 'Though hearts may meet in greeting, bodies will sink into sin' was a phrase she often repeated. She was one of the first girls at school to substitute the Islamic expression 'God's peace upon you', an unusual greeting at the time, for the simple 'good morning'. She believed that all those who refused to pronounce God's peace in greeting sullied their hearts. She was constantly preoccupied with sin, constantly reading about it, parsing and interpreting it, and hunting for the definitive bibliography of commentaries that would make her alone the possessor of its true meaning. She started a preaching meeting at school with a few fellow classmates. She had a genius for making the other girls cry and feel the heavy burden of their guilt — any guilt. It made her spirits soar to see them in tears because her own long road began and ended in tears. While the other girls were busy with the school radio station and the wall newspapers and all the other extra-curricular activities, she lowered her eyes and stifled her desires and went on acting the part of a great heroine, an instrument of God. For a long time, she really believed herself to be just that.

But in the same way that she had been the first girl to put on that long black curtain, she was the first one to discard it. Now she began to claim that modesty and beauty could comfortably coexist in God's eyes. She entered into a long, confusing period during which she dug around once again for the commentaries and legal opinions that would support her about-face with textual evidence that she could interpret as she liked. She was still busy being different. She exchanged the loose robes that she used to drag behind her in the dust for others that were shorter, tighter, and more flattering to the curves of her body: bright, colourful dresses whose sinfulness had yet to be proven beyond a shadow of a doubt. She unleashed a strategic strand of hair from beneath her headscarf, because God is merciful and compassionate and He would surely not consider her strand of hair to be a mortal sin. Here she is now, walking down Flatbush Avenue completely bare-headed, and no one is so much as glancing at her. But her eyes are still lowered out of habit. Her timid glances are the product of years of fear and frustration. She still wears loose clothes because her body is less than perfect; the flaccid figure of a middle-aged woman whose hair is caught up in a severe bun just because she can't find the time to do it properly. She has to run around all day after the bus, to the market, to her son's school. The Latina women walking down the same street are dressed in tight skirts and pretty, revealing tops or short-shorts, and no one bothers to look at them. They stretch out on the green grass of Prospect Park and their naked thighs lie open to the sun.

✳

Hend crosses the Park on her way to the library every day. She sits on the wide stone steps waiting for her English class to begin. Said sits next to her, smiling sweetly. She inspects the sweetness in his eyes and isn't sure how to interpret it. She looks at the vertical scar on his cheek and the tattoo on his chin, and she remembers that her father had a similar scar in the same place because he grew up at a time when bloodletting was the only treatment for any number of ailments. She doesn't understand why he has a tattoo, though: tattoos are for women, but it makes Said's smile seem broader and more inviting. Said always wears dark suits because he's a limousine driver. Sometimes he shares his halva or falafel sandwiches with her before class or after. These impromptu snacks are often interrupted by sudden telephone calls. He answers politely: 'Yes, Father. Okay, Father.' Afterwards he explains to her that his parish priest wants him to do some volunteer work at the church. Said has never told her how he ended up in America. He has spoken only about his many relatives, the lottery, and the church's charitable work, and one day he shyly invites her on an outing: 'Why don't you come and spend a Sunday with us and then we can go for a walk afterwards?' She accepts because she likes his boyish, comical manner, and because he really seems to enjoy her company. It is something she needs: someone to care for her, someone she might possibly love and be loved by; something to hold on to should everything else crumble away. Hend often glimpses the ghostly features of her only true friend in Said's face. This friend was born in the House of Capricorn. He had loved her sincerely and he died simply. She likes being with Said because he is kind and says sweet things to her. He reminds her of all the people she has cared for in her life.

The only church that Hend ever knew as a child was an unfinished structure that stood between the Hill Estate and Pharaoh's Hills. On her way to the schoolroom built by Mr Wadi on top of the hill she always passed a few scattered houses. Mr Wadi was the French teacher and he was married to Miss Ellen, the chemistry teacher, who had a small cross tattooed between her eyebrows. More and more teachers from the outside world came to Pharaoh's Hills. They always settled in and around the far-flung and inexpensive area near the schools. Mr Wadi's house was next door to Doctor Shamil the pharmacist's house and also to the houses of Mr Mina, the Greek jeweller, and Madame Teresa, the seamstress. More teachers came to Pharaoh's Hills at the beginning of every school year: Mr Samir Girgis, the math teacher, was one of them. Their houses huddled together in an intimate circle. The schoolroom sat on top of the hill, solitary and white. It was built of mud and plaster and it was bare but for a few chairs. Sometimes it smelled of burned candles. Outside there were a few trees and a large metal sign: 'Permit to build the Mother of Light

Church on the Muqawi Estate, district capital of Pharaoh's Hills'. Nearby, the Nur Mosque – also known as the Kuwaiti Mosque – would soon be born. It was named after the Kuwaiti sheikh who donated the funds for its construction. The mosque stood high and proud, with a tall minaret and marble steps and green carpets and taps that spouted cold water in summer. The town had never seen anything so luxurious before, but the small hill had trouble accommodating two buildings consecrated to God in such a tight space. The Mother of Light Church was consumed by fire every few months and rebuilt every time. After each fire, fights would break out. Mr Wadi and some of his neighbours always took part in these brawls. The road to Mr Wadi's house bristled with security details and was littered with broken pieces of coloured glass from the windows of both buildings. New paths sprouted up on the hill and Hend began to avoid the area altogether. She still doesn't know if the Mother of Light Church was ever finished.

These are the memories of Pharaoh's Hills that have stayed with her. Everything else she's forgotten, because she now forgets a lot of things. She often leaves the food to burn on the stove and the smoke alarm disturbs her neighbours. She doesn't quite understand how she's stumbled into old age so suddenly and without warning.

Said picks her up in his limousine. He sits next to her in the big church with the high ceiling and she listens politely. The priest stands in front of her, neat and smiling in a simple grey suit, and welcomes her warmly, as does everyone else. They shake her hand energetically and introduce themselves without any fuss. They make her feel that she has always been one of them. She smiles politely and stands up when they do and sits down when they do. She nods her head at them and returns their smiles in kind. She listens closely to the sermon.

One day a man approached Christ to ask about his future. 'You will die when your oldest son reaches the age of twenty-five,' the Lord replied. The man, who did not have a son, wept, for he didn't want to die. Fearing the prophecy, he avoided marriage altogether and lived alone, never going near any woman. One day a young man knocked on his door and begged leave to spend the night, as he was a traveller. In the morning, the young man shook his sleeping host and found him dead. Twenty years later, the young man discovered that the kind host who had taken him in and died on the morrow was his father.

Hend has heard different versions of this story, but she can't remember where or when. She muses on its significance. It seems to be saying that man is a pitiful creature. As far as Hend is concerned, there was no need for Christ or any other prophet to prove this truth. She nods her head wisely. The parable has moved her and she wants the others to see this. The man in the grey suit descends from the pulpit and shakes her hand again enthusiastically. He sits next to her and another priest takes his place in the pulpit. He too wears a grey suit and a wide smile, and he welcomes her publicly to the church. The congregation all turn to stare at her and smile. She is getting tired of all these smiles and nodding heads and decides to change the expression on her face to one of mute indifference. The second priest says, 'A traveller met a wise man and asked him for counsel. The wise man pointed to his heart and said, "Cultivate therein three things: modesty and the knowledge of sin, fear, and lastly courage, for if a heart understands not sin it will never change, and if it feels no fear it will discover no need to change, and if it possesses not courage it will be incapable of changing.'" Hend used to believe that she had managed to exorcise the ghost of sin that had accompanied her throughout her childhood and youth, and that she had finally freed herself of her fear, but she realised long ago that this was untrue. As she is making up her mind to leave, the hymns begin, rising from the lips of the congregation in powerful waves of sound.

In the corridors leading to the room where lunch has been laid out, she examines the pictures of Christian missions in familiar places: the alleys of Sohag, the neighbourhoods of Darfur. A feeling of listlessness and despair creeps over her. It appears that the only man ever to ask her out in New York is trying to convert her. She feels nothing looking at the images of children who resemble her own son crowding around the milk cartons and relief supplies. She feels that she is nothing but an indefinite noun, a pitiful anonymity, a woman solitary and neglected, sitting by herself at the far corner of a table. Said sits next to her; Said, whom she had imagined – only imagined – was in love with her. The thought had made her happy, because she wanted to imagine that someone was in love with her. Said smiles and laughs as he exchanges pleasantries with friends and neighbours. She eats slowly, mechanically, never taking her eyes off the hamburger on her paper plate. She smiles absently as the memory of Angele and the halva sandwich comes floating back to her. She wonders if she's turning into a version of Angele, a plump woman with short hair, crushed by fear, seeking out imaginary walls to flatten herself against. Pluto is facing her down for the next few years, after all. The house she grew up in, the familiar houses of neighbours, have vanished into the thin air of time. Her only vista now is the endless corridor of Flatbush Avenue, twisting and turning into alien side streets.

She leaves just as she came. She gets into the car with Said. She notices that he seems unusually cheerful.

'How come you're in such a good mood?' she asks him timidly.

'I'm always happy, as my name says.'

'How lucky for you.'

'If a person has faith, they'll always be happy.'

She feels as if she's heard this before. She's heard it a lot, heard it and even repeated it herself many times. But she feigns innocence, to please him.

'Faith in what?' she asks stupidly.

'In God, of course.'

The look on his face leads her to worry that he's about to start preaching in earnest. She suddenly realises that he has prepared his catechism in advance, thinking to change her life, to save her from herself, but she alone knows that in this lesson lies her destruction. She struggles to evoke a cord of empathy with which to bind this stranger to her. She gazes at the vertical scar on his face.

'Do you know that you're the first man to ask me out in this city?' she murmurs wistfully. She hopes to soften his heart and to make him see her as a woman.

He smiles and avoids her eyes.

She continues, 'I want to feel free tonight. Free from expectations of any kind. Free to save myself in my own way, free to be myself. Do you know what that means?'

She laughs and throws her head back coyly on the passenger seat of the limousine, but he doesn't say anything. She suggests they take a walk so that she can tell him more, but she's all wound up now; she feels hurt and also offended. She would have thrown herself into his arms if he'd asked her to, would have stayed next to him in the car forever, with no shame. Her excitement is cosmic. Mars has recently moved into her zodiac, adding layers of cruel impetuosity to her usual anxiety. Said is unmoved. She tells him the story of her grandmother the Guest as they sit eating ice cream on Seventh Avenue, but he is restrained and uncomfortable, an insipid smile plastered on his face.

She watches his car move away down the long dark street, then she goes into Coco Bar – the bar below her apartment – and orders a beer. She regrets not having told him her father's story instead: maybe it would have been more effective. She reproaches herself for not having given him the opportunity to be a hero: men have their dream roles too, she muses sadly. Now she feels unbearably heavy with a longing to open up and talk. She looks around her. Most of the customers in the bar are women sitting by themselves, like her. She wonders who listens to the stories spinning around in dusty corners of their brains.

She remembers her father sitting on the mat in the eastern balcony surrounded by camphor and tamarisk trees. He was telling how Noah spoke from his ark to his son, who was standing on the mountain that would save him from the deluge: 'There is no protection from God's judgment, save for those who have earned His mercy.' The eastern balcony lay wide open to the sky. Hend was rubbing her father's feet. His head lay in her mother's lap. Stars shone down on the circle that her brothers formed around him. They were all close to each other in age, except for the oldest, who had grown tall and proud of his small beard. He disappeared into God's way for a few days every month and his mother would say, 'He's studying,' because she refused to believe that the handsome, gentle son who used to collect stamps and play the harmonica and devour comic books had become an Islamist. Little Hend didn't understand why he came up the steps that led to the eastern balcony with those deliberate, epic strides that day and screamed in her father's face: 'Shame on you! It's forbidden – what you're doing is a sin!'

Their father raised his head from his wife's lap and sat up. The younger brothers, who were all engrossed in the story of Noah, looked at each other and then at their big brother. Their father tapped his knee with his fingers in a silent drumbeat of fury. He didn't say a word and the oldest son, tall and skinny in his spotlessly white scented jalaba, ran away, shouting an expression that he'd learned by heart: 'May God curse the one who drinks it or traffics in it or buys it.' He hid in the pantry and cried alone amongst the sacks piled up in the corners and the odour of mouldy wheat. He cried like a small, terrified child. 'I'm afraid that he'll go to hell, Mother. You know how much I love him.' Their father withdrew into his room, leaning on little Hend's shoulder. 'Are you sad, Papa?' she asked him. He didn't reply. He lay down on his bed and turned on the small radio on the nightstand to listen to the BBC news bulletin.

She massaged his tired feet, as he liked her to do. Her palm was small and frail and comforting. With each stroke she tried to dissipate the unnatural fog of silence that enveloped him. Their mother came in, leading her oldest son, still crying, by the hand. Their father smiled when he saw him, then he suddenly burst out laughing as though just at that moment discovering that this young man was his firstborn child. Her brother hung his head and said, 'I'm afraid for you, Papa.' Their father smiled. 'The mountain will save me from the waters.' The son replied with a practised formula to prove his claim: '"That thing of which much intoxicates is forbidden even in the smallest quantity."' Their father smiled again. '"A little of it strengthens the heart and does away with sorrow." Do you know who said that? The famously strict jurist Ahmad ibn Hanbal. Which means that you're more of a Hanbali than Ibn Hanbal himself.' Her eldest brother cried and her father laughed. He'd found his sense of humour again now, and was insisting that beer was 'a great pharaonic invention'. Then he went to sleep, complaining of a pain in his left shoulder.

Many years later, his daughter sits in a small bar in a neighbourhood of Brooklyn. She stares at the foam in her glass, the white bubbles popping as they settle on its surface. The pretty young bartender looks at her sympathetically. She asks about her son. 'Where's the cute little man who I always see you with?' Hend smiles at the question and points to the ceiling of the bar, above which the boy lies on his bed waiting for her to come home.

Hend sleeps a lot because she is always tired, because she is all alone, and because she doesn't have anything particular to do. She pulls the covers over her face to hide her exhaustion from him. He snuggles up to her as he watches drawn faces like her own talking on the TV screen. 'The signs of depression are constant fatigue, irritability, apathy, feelings of sadness, and suicidal thoughts. Ask your doctor about treatment. Depression is painful. Ask your doctor about Cymbalta. Cymbalta can help.' He watches the faces in the commercial as they materialise and then fade into nothing. He shakes her under the covers. 'Mom, sometimes you don't answer me when I talk to you and you act sad – *very sad*,' he repeats in English.

'So?' she asks wearily.

'You should go see a doctor. You might die!'

'Don't worry.'

'But if you do die, for example, what would happen to me?'

'You'd go back to Egypt.'

'But I don't want to go back to Egypt.'

'We have to go back sometime.'

'Why do we have to? If you're not happy here you could take Cymbalta, or go to the doctor.'

She buries her head in the pillow and laughs. He doesn't like it when she laughs at him. He turns his face away angrily, and she burrows her head deep under the pillow and goes to sleep.

6

Tango

She hears his footsteps on the stairs, and wonders how one person can make all that noise. The first time she saw him in the building he was standing on the landing in front of her door. He had tripped over her son's bicycle and dropped the carton of bottles that he was carrying. When she opened the door, he was picking up the pieces of broken glass that had scattered all over the landing and cursing the landlord and the tenants and anyone else he could think of. She quietly took her son's bicycle inside and shut the door, leaving him to figure out how to clean up the spilled beer. The smell of alcohol lingered on her floor for a long time after, the smell of hops and beery foam, as well as a few tiny shards of broken glass. The second time he saw her he tried to be more pleasant. He said that the landlord rarely rented apartments to families with children and that he was glad she and her son had moved in — it made the building seem more cheerful. She nodded as she looked at the dark, narrow stairs and breathed in the strong wood smell that rose from the old banister. As he talked, she looked everywhere but at him, then she quietly went up to her apartment.

He lives in the apartment right above hers. Every time he goes up or down the stairs he always has a carton of bottles with him. He wears a baseball cap and rides around on a bicycle that he locks up on the ground floor of the building. He lives alone. She guessed this from the slow, rhythmic sound of his footsteps tapping above her every night. She has come to know the sound of his hurried steps on the stairs too, what time he goes to work, and what time he comes back. She knows that he eavesdrops on the tenants with those sharp ears of his. Whenever she meets him on the stairs, he says the same thing: 'Did you hear the ruckus in the building yesterday? That band and the loud music? I have no idea why the landlord rents to crazy people like that. I can't sleep in this building! Children, live music, bizarre neighbours . . .'

She leaves him cursing and complaining and goes into her apartment. She knows for a fact that he has his own share of bizarre visitors, such as that petite woman who comes to see him from time to time. She locks up her bike next to his and climbs the stairs with a six-pack of beer. When she comes to visit, the loud music moves from the apartment next door to the one upstairs – his apartment – and drowns out the rhythmic noise of their love making. The climax of their sighs and moans floats in and out of the regular, booming beat above her head. She turns up her TV or the AC but she can never sleep until the battle upstairs is finally over. The woman always leaves at midnight on the dot. She descends the stairs with the empty beer bottles, which she throws in the garbage chute, then takes her bike and rides off into the night.

Occasionally the tiny fair-skinned woman disappears for days, and sometimes weeks, and then he enters into a period of absolute silence. During these periods she rarely hears the sound of his footsteps above her, just the rush of water flushing in the toilet or the clanking of pots and pans in the kitchen. She smells the odour of coffee coming from his open window. She knows that his bed is exactly above her own, and when he tosses and turns she pictures him mumbling restlessly in his sleep.

During these periods of hibernation, Hend turns her attention to her downstairs neighbour. She has woven a story out of the young woman's comings and goings and her boyfriend's visits. The smell of tacos drifts up to her from the downstairs window.

Hend draws perverse comfort from the cheerless building. She takes pleasure in sharing intimate moments with anonymous, unsuspecting people; people who surely recognise the timbre of her voice when she yells at her son and the sound of water bubbling and purring in her pipe at night. They know that she sleeps alone, and that she talks in her sleep. She always leaves the TV on at night because she is afraid of the silence. Her next-door neighbours know her son's name and which school he attends. They see her crossing the street with him every morning. They know what time she washes the dishes every day, and recognise the smell of tea with cloves wafting out from her window in the evenings. They know the sound of her laugh and the nights when insomnia stalks her: the nights when she lies awake, terrified that her heart might suddenly stop beating and that she'll be forced to leave behind forever the young boy peacefully asleep in his bed. She imagines him rubbing his eyes awake in the morning, then shaking her cold, rigid body in a growing crescendo of terror. She has scrawled the names and numbers of all the people she knows in Brooklyn on the kitchen wall – Emilia, Said, Fatima – and she keeps his passport visible on the kitchen table. That way anyone who finds him could send him to his father. He would simply pick up his passport and go back, leaving her body for the landlord and the police to deal with, and the Refugee Aid Society would toss it into any old cemetery.

She hears footsteps from the old wooden stairwell. She knows they aren't her upstairs neighbour's heavy steps. She recognises them: they belong to his blonde lady friend. But the tiny woman doesn't keep going up the next flight of stairs to his apartment. She stops at her apartment. Hend waits for the knock, and when she opens the door she notices that the woman's nose is red and swollen. Up close, she looks to be in her late forties or early fifties. She holds a little girl by the hand, about the same age as her own son. 'Excuse me for barging in on you like this,' she says tersely, as though they've known each other for a long time. 'Could I leave my daughter with you for a few minutes? I have to talk to him. I'll be right back.' Then she sprints up the stairs. The girl, who seems very wise for her age, steps inside as though being taken in charge by a stranger is the most usual of circumstances, something that happens to her every day. She walks into the room and sits down next to the boy, who is busy watching TV. They don't exchange a word at first. They just sit there and watch the cartoons for a while. Finally, they begin to talk as though they had been sitting on that couch together since the day they were born.

'Do you like SpongeBob?' she asks.

'He's funny.'

'I like Iron Man. What about Hannah Montana?'

'Girls always like Hannah Montana. Isn't that silly?'

This minor difference of opinion quickly turns into a sharp

exchange accompanied by an anxious swinging of legs, and words like 'dumb', 'stupid', and 'freaky' fly around the room. They were two kids who had never laid eyes on each other before, then suddenly discovered that they were sharing a couch and decided to make the best of it.

She is still observing them intently when the knock comes again at the door. The tiny blonde woman is back. Her nose is still red from crying and there is no mistaking the miserable expression on her face. She speaks in the same neutral tone. 'Excuse me again. Can you call my daughter? Thanks.' The girl leaves quietly, just as she had come. They descend the narrow wooden staircase together and disappear forever. No more will she see her going up or coming down, or hear her athletic body bouncing on the bed right above her head. After that, her upstairs neighbour's movements grow slower than usual. Even the sound of running water in his bathroom trickles into nothing. She wonders whether he has moved out of the building altogether, or killed himself. Utter silence reigns above the ceiling of her room. It takes him a long time to return to his normal self. She starts seeing him again as she leads her son by the hand to school. She sees him parking his bike downstairs and carrying the six-pack of beer up to his apartment late at night. Sometimes they meet by chance and he will nod at her briefly. Once in a while he'll say a few words: 'The weather is gorgeous today' or 'How's your son? Does he like New York?'

✳

The spring breezes pass over Flatbush Avenue and her son spends more and more of his time playing chess and watching Iron Man and SpongeBob on TV. Every evening, for an hour or so, she sits outside the building on the wooden bench in front of Coco Bar and watches the world go by on the broad avenue. The bench is frequented by smokers and dog-walkers, or joggers catching their breath after a long run. She sits alone and watches the passers-by, drinking coffee and smoking her cigarette. Her upstairs neighbour passes by and stops to chat. 'Do you like to dance? Have you ever tried tango or salsa?' She gets the impression that he's asking her out on a date. She sees his face up close for the first time. He looked to be about sixty, but the setting sun makes him look older in spite of his tall, athletic build. She tries to smile in response to his friendly question. 'I'd like to, but I've never had the chance. I didn't even dance on my wedding day. I sat on a chair and watched my husband dance with every one of my friends.' He chuckles at this, and she realises that there's more to him than meets the eye. She finds out that his name is Charlie. 'There are schools for dancing, you know.' He hands her a card and says that he's a dance instructor and that he'd be happy to give her some lessons — for free, of course. She nods her head. 'Alright, maybe,' she murmurs. She is growing tired of watching other people living. She decides that maybe it's time to start colouring her hair again and getting out a bit.

The first time she goes to the spacious dance studio with the gleaming parquet floor she feels a thrill at seeing her face, smiling and happy, reflected back at her in so many mirrors. She stares at the body that was a stranger to her. Ever since the day of her first period, her body has been an obscure question mark. Unlike her girlfriends, for her the onset of puberty came relatively late. In class the girls talked about their cramps and the flow of blood and compared the size of their growing breasts. Hend always tried to make herself invisible in these gatherings; she feigned total indifference, even though she had memorised the entire chapter on reproductive anatomy in her biology textbook. The biology teacher said, 'I'm not going to explain this particular lesson in class. Read it at home.' The girls giggled in low voices. The drawings of the male reproductive organs in the book astonished and frightened them. The chapter was at the very end, after the chapters on the digestive, respiratory, and nervous systems. It was appended to the chapter on cell division. Normal everyday words took on unprecedented sexual meanings: 'the tube'; 'the socket'; 'male and female'. But the words that unsettled Hend most were the ones that came from her geography book: innocent words like 'topography' and 'plains and valleys' suddenly began to give off the smell of sex. She quickly discovered that she was the only one of her classmates who hadn't yet been visited by 'the sculptor of girls' – that master craftsman of folk legend who chisels out the curves of waists and breasts and bellies and buttocks, adding a touch here and there to the planes of the face, along with a smattering of pimples.

When her period finally came, it was brown, like coffee; just a few dark spots she discovered in her underwear. Later, it was like rivers of dark red blood, and she had to use loads of those cloth rags that her mother kept hidden in the bathroom. A single swollen pimple appeared on the tip of her nose every month. It would come and then go, and her body would return to normal, her face resuming its placid roundness. She began to develop a new relationship with her bodily fluids. She became obsessed with fantastic love stories and poems about solitude and longing and passionate embraces. She took perverse pleasure in the explosive fits of weeping that came over her, and in contemplating the mysterious rhythms produced by her hormones and the pimples full of watery pus. She did not love her body and she had never thought about it much before. She came to understand that the violent emotions that seized her were cyclic, tied to the paired ebb and flow of hormones and planets. Hers was a water sign: she was born to be curious, timid, dreamy, and delusional. It was a pretty hopeless sign all in all, despite its tendency to selflessness and empathy.

Hend's periods stopped when she was thirty-three years old, for reasons that she understood only later. On a day like all the others, she came out of her bedroom holding the baby's bottle; the baby who slept curled in a ball between them on the bed that smelled of talcum powder and saliva, of urine and sweat and vomit, of medicines for fever and indigestion. The bedspread was covered with stains, and patches of desiccated milk spotted her blouse. She went into the kitchen and put the water and anise leaves in the kettle. As she waited for the tea to boil she wandered into his study and began to poke around in his open desk drawer. Her hand immediately fell upon a packet of letters. All she remembers now from those letters are a few passionate phrases that he had written to some woman or other. The baby began to cry, the tea boiled over and the milk in her breast burned. She went back into the bedroom and tore up the letters into tiny pieces over his sleeping, twitching body, then she began to hit him with both her hands. 'Get up! Get out! I don't want to see you in this house ever again.'

So he left, and then he came back with angry excuses. The 'lapse' became a string of repeated lapses, and they ceased to shock her. The bouts of hysterical weeping turned to stony silence, and the silence to repulsion. Then the repulsion became a hard, resigned detachment. It was during this time that her periods became shorter and less frequent, and Hend discovered that the sticky liquid – that irritating guest – was deeply connected to her body's well-being, much like the milk that seeped out from her nipples at inexplicable and inconvenient times.

✳

The dance studio is panelled with mirrors. She can see her body clearly in them. She ponders the old scar underneath her eyes, the one that used to make her feel shy all the time, the one that she was always trying to hide in her childhood. She would stand in front of the mirror and place her hand on her cheek to erase it from the image in the glass. She tried yogurt-and-honey face masks, and all kinds of exfoliating creams. After each experiment, the image looking back at her from the mirror would be sharper. She pored over the beauty pages in magazines and diligently researched the best concealing foundations. In later years it became more pronounced, like a scabby wound stamped on her cheek right under the eye, an area that all the beauty experts warned was especially sensitive. Every year she would note with surprise that the scar had gotten worse, and that, as the wrinkles accumulated on her face, it became a broad convex arc. She told herself sardonically that it was her very own beauty mark and that it made her face unforgettable.

And she actually began to believe it. She took to decorating it with a tiny pencilled mole – a mole like the one the voluptuous actress Mimi Shakib wore in old Egyptian movies, a perfectly round mole that looked like a stain spreading miserably inside the scar. She rubbed in more foundation creams and thought about getting it surgically removed. Maybe she would get a nose job and collagen injections for her lips while she was at it. Perhaps she should pluck her eyebrows to give them a nice high arch. That would mean she'd have to change the colour of her hair and her contact lenses too. Her dreams of a brand-new body never materialised, of course. Her belly grew big with the baby and she spent all her time after that chasing after the crawling infant and feeding him and poring over the resemblance between his little face and her grown one: the same receding upper lip, the same slightly prominent nose and thick eyebrows joined at the middle. He would put his hand on her scar and ask, 'What's this, Mama?' When she hugged him she discovered that the curves of his spine and his fingers were shaped exactly like hers. Her child feels her scar with his palm and kisses it, then runs off to grow up on his own, leaving her behind. She frets about her body's other imperfections – the flabby flesh around her stomach, the muscles grown slack from pregnancy and childbirth.

She examines her body as though she's never seen it before. She ponders its little scars and defects, all more noticeable now in the short dress she's wearing: stitches in the knee after falling off a swing at her uncle's house, a break in the right arm when

88

she'd climbed their front gate in one of her attempts to escape, a burn on the back of her hand from the first time she'd fried potatoes, droopy eyelids from plucking the brows over and over, rolls of flesh around the stomach that used to be tight-knit bands of muscle holding him firmly in place when he was a fetus, the old scar under her eye. She watches her face moving through all those mirrors: features stripped of all their usual veils, wrinkled by the months and years, leaving Hend with the profound feeling that her life is now all behind her.

Charlie takes her by the hand and begins to teach her the first steps: 'One, two, three, four.' He is unusually tall and he doesn't move like an old man at all. His body is sinewy and graceful. She turns in circles a few times, getting her steps mixed up, not knowing where to look — at her feet or at the mirrors? Or at his face? He moves amongst the students in the group, pulling them close to him one by one, as though they were all his lovers: 'One, two, three, four.' Everyone settles into the rhythmic movements — she is the only one who keeps making the same mistakes, and the knowledge of it makes her even more confused and clumsy. The dance seems to her like a string of mistakes repeated with the same obstinate stupidity. It is exactly like her life: a game in which two people come together and move apart according to strict rules regulating momentum and balance. She can't quite grasp the requisite equilibrium and she stumbles again and again. She has never liked the game in real life and she doesn't like it as a formal dance either. She just cannot bring herself to let a man take her by the hand and hold her in his arms, and she cannot believe that all she has to do is to respond slowly and gracefully. A step back and a step forward. She turns in helpless circles and loses her balance. She suspects that everyone is laughing at her. She tries to watch what the other dancers are doing. She feels ashamed of the smell of sweat coming from her armpits. She wonders whether the bulkiness of her torso makes her less agile. Her legs are too stiff to execute the sudden dips and twirls properly and she suddenly feels infinitely tired.

After class, she walks back home with Charlie. As they talk, she has the strange feeling that she's met him before. Here, away from the dance floor, he reminds her of a frog – of all the men in her life that she has never really liked. She wonders at the chameleon-like nature of men. She remembers the first time she actually saw her husband cheating on her. She hates that word, 'cheating'. It makes her think of old Zahrit al-Ula movies. Zahrit al-Ula always played the role of the tearful, deceived wife who lived in the shadows and talked a lot about virtue and self-respect. Hend detested the wife role: real heroines were never wives. Mistresses in movies were a lot more appealing. They had plunging necklines and wide, glittering eyes that could hold a gaze without blinking. But Hend doubts that she has ever been suited for the role of leading lady. She just isn't qualified. That's why her favourite old movie is *The Well of Privation*, where the heroine commits every kind of sin in her dreams at night, then wakes up in the morning fresh and unsullied.

She tells Charlie all about the first time she saw her husband flirting with another woman. It happened in her own house and the woman was her friend. All his mistresses were her friends – or plotted to become her friends after the fact. She still doesn't understand what the point was. She remembers the evening clearly. She was wearing a pretty new dress and moving gaily around the room, full of that glowing self-assurance that only fools live on. The guests were heatedly discussing something – what, she can't recall. She didn't know any of their faces, had never seen them before. Her husband, meanwhile, was engaged in a different type of conversation. Her friend had been dancing alone to an old Umm Kulthum song. Hend had always loved that particular melody and they often listened to it together as the friend told her stories about the early days of her first marriage and her life since. She sat down opposite Hend's husband and they began to steal long, languorous glances at each other. It wasn't difficult for Hend to see that her husband knew this woman well, that he had handled her body and whispered to her in the arrogant and lewd accents of masculine possession. Hend was as good at reading these signs and tokens as she was at stuffing cabbage leaves or pigeons and making rice casseroles. She was like Zahrit al-Ula in the old movies. She watched the brazen, defiant exchange that dared everyone to notice. They could all see what was going on right in front of their noses. But people like to share in little conspiracies. The truth remains unsaid and the unsaid is, when all's said and done, immaterial.

Hend recalls the scene unfolding. Her friend went over to the buffet and her husband followed her and picked at the hors d'oeuvres. Then his hand reached out to stroke the cleft between her breasts, and she shivered and laughed nervously. Hend was just coming out of the kitchen with a tray of finger food, but she pretended that she hadn't seen anything. She just turned and walked straight back into the kitchen. 'The way of the world,' she whispered to herself, just as her mother had taught her. It's true that this had all happened rather early in her married life, but what did that matter? All men were the same, weren't they? It was the first time her husband had appeared repulsive and obscene to her, and also the first time that she had felt unbearably stupid and terribly slow. Incidents like these multiplied and the snapshots she stored in her head became clearer and sharper. The violent confrontations grew more frequent – confrontations in which he always denied everything, because denial is the fuel of conspiracy. He accused her of being crazy. Hend turned in circles, frantically looking for his missing underwear and socks. She spent her days searching for proof of his infidelities, but whenever she found something, pretending that everything was fine became that much harder and her need to flee that much more urgent. She began to avoid him entirely.

In the beginning she took her frustration out on the pillows, as though they alone were the cause of her misery. She went through terrible mood swings – shrinking from his body in disgust and then making passionate love to him. She began to hate the mattress that they slept on. It had belonged to him before they married, and those dark stains and musty smells had not been made by her. Yes, she knew the way of the world now: knew, as her mother had taught her, that a man's only disgrace was the size of his wallet, and yet she clung fiercely to her madness. She stitched up a brand-new clean white cotton mattress that she could call her own, and tossed and turned on it with her heavy, bloated belly.

Charlie listens to her without a word. Does he even understand what she is saying? Maybe her accent is too thick. Or maybe he just isn't interested. She starts to tell him about her nightmares.

She sees her friends, and sometimes the men she's secretly loved, clasping hands and forming a circle around her. Each one tries to touch her in turn. The game is called Blind Bear. She is the only person wearing a blindfold; she is the dim-witted one. She runs panting after the shadows that form in the inky darkness. The Blind Bear turns round and round, frantically searching for the hands that push her from behind. She cocks her ear to catch the loud voices that surround her. She whirls her stick in the air to measure the empty space. She tries to avoid the groping hands that seek her. They push her and she falls, over and over. The game ends when she finally begs for mercy. They make a circle around her and taunt her: 'The Blind Bear's fallen into the well!' The well is deep and her fall is exhilarating. She falls, over and over, endlessly. She always wakes up from this dream in utter panic. The Blind Bear is dim-witted and makes the same mistakes over and over. She falls in love with the same man over and over. She believes that all she has to do is bend so as not to break. It's hard for her to say these things to Charlie because she doesn't know how to translate them into his language. She hopes he has understood.

She could hear the sound of water splashing on her husband's body in the bathroom. She pictured his naked body moving around as he shaved and picked out his clothes. He sang in his room. He sang with the pure delight of a man in love. She waited till she heard the front door shut behind him before coming out from her room to take a warm bath. She breathed a sigh of relief. She decided that she wouldn't even bother to tell him that she was leaving on a trip and maybe never coming back, and that she didn't love him any more – that his presence in this world wounded her. She wished that she could force him to take off his clothes – the clothes that smelled of another woman – before he came into her house. Sometimes she sniffed them all over for that smell. But she didn't care in the end; she just wanted to know the truth, to convince herself that she had plumbed his depths. She knew where he hid his letters and when he came in his dreams as she lay sleeping next to him. She was quite familiar with the sticky, foul-smelling stains on his underwear and she understood why he was always leaving them around for her to find. She knew why he always kept his cell phone close to him, in his pocket or under his pillow at night. On that day he had left it on the edge of the dresser. She turned the sleeping phone over in her hands as she waited for the tub to fill with water. She stood there for a long time, lost in thought, then decided to turn it on and read the messages. She still experienced a feeling of utter panic at moments like these. The clean, warm water caressed her body. The phone beckoned. She knew that the PIN code was made up of the letters of her name. After a few tries she got the right combination and scrolled through to the inbox with its long list of messages. She already knew what she would find there: promised kisses, obscene whispers, and postponed meetings. She drowned the phone in the bathwater to erase its memory once and for all.

Charlie pats her shoulder and smiles sympathetically, then he gives her a quick kiss on the cheek and runs up the stairs to his apartment.

*

The women taking classes with Hend at the dance studio dress in long, flowery skirts like the ones Zahrit al-Ula wore in the movies. They clutch scented handkerchiefs and wear high-heeled shoes. Each woman seems to turn in circles around her own failures. The music is always sad, and the lyrics are about weeping women and the men who abandoned them. The sticky, sweaty palms of her dance partners leave her cold and unmoved. At the end of the lesson everybody turns their backs on everybody else and walks off in different directions. Charlie stays behind with her only because they live in the same building and he feels obliged to walk her home. As they walk next to each other, he tells her that he started dancing after his first divorce because he wanted to learn how to gauge the proper distance between a man and a woman; to learn the exact point of balance between desire and retreat, intimacy and habit. Hend nods her head. She had never danced with a man before. When Charlie danced he seemed much younger than he really was, and as he talks she can hardly believe that he is the same man who drags his bike along angrily every morning, cursing the building and its tenants. He explains the history of the dance to her. He tells her that it began with the first wail unleashed by the prisoners in the slave ships, then its rhythms were picked up by the Spaniards who crossed the seas. It was the same lecture he gave all his students. She realises nonetheless that he is deliberately trying to be charming as she walks by his side demurely. When he puts his arm around her, her unexpectedly firm reply surprises her. 'I hope you don't mind my saying this, but please don't do that.' Does he understand? Does he put her rejection of him down to

95

some kind of radical cultural difference? She leaves a wider space between them after that as they walk: that hypothetical distance that he is always talking about in class, a distance that begs for uncomplicated sympathy.

Charlie tells her that the tango is a dance of longing. She likes this way of putting it. 'Why do you love me?' she had once asked her first love long ago (a question that women often ask to gauge the measure of their uniqueness in their lover's eyes). 'Do you know that Fairuz song?' he replied, '"I'm Yearning for Someone Whose Face I've Never Seen"?' That was all he said. He left her to translate and she came to the conclusion that, as far as he was concerned, their relationship was nothing but the whisper of an obscure longing, like the longing of Charlie's Spaniards. Back then his words had wounded her deeply, but she later realised that this vague, objectless longing was also part of the way of the world. The other women in the dance studio are living examples of this dictum. They have crossed over gently into their thirties. Little wrinkles have begun to sprout at the edges of their faces. She can see them sitting, like her, at windows overlooking some avenue or other, calmly watching life pass by and aching to become a part of it. The tango was a kind of therapy that helped them understand the basic rules of love and life, rules whose time was slowly expiring: distance, attraction, and balance.

The dance resembles the game of love. The world retreats as the partner moves in, then rushes forward again as he turns his back and moves away with choreographed steps. The act of coming together and moving apart precisely and deliberately creates an exact distance between solitary bodies that is the notional space of union. The man approaches this space cautiously. He gently reaches out and takes the woman's hand in his with confidence and desire. 'Relax in his embrace. Let him lead you. Let him decide when to pull you close and push you away in a single, graceful movement.' The tango, Charlie says, is the philosophy of shared space. She discovers that most of the other students, both men and women, have been recently divorced; the question of distance perplexes them too.

The second time that she and Charlie walk home together she feels the need to talk and talk. She feels that she has gotten to know him better, that his face has grown familiar to her. It no longer reminds her of a frog's face. Now he looks more like a greyhound, with slender, well-proportioned limbs made for running races, or a fantastic creature in an animated film. He reminds her of herself, too, because he is alone and wretched just like her, crushed by the noise of a building in which other people made love as he lay alone in bed at night, listening. He holds out a glass of white wine to her and they sit down on the bench outside the Coco Bar. It is hot. His forehead is wet with perspiration and she can feel it staining the underarms of her blouse. She tells him that she is a Cancer. 'Do you know that Cancer is notoriously bad at finding its balance?' She tells him that Cancers are like the Blind Bear, falling in love for no reason. Cancers also like to close their eyes and run after their one true love. As a child she had been really good at playing hide-and-seek, running, running away, then finding herself standing all alone, hiding in the shade of a wall. No one ever noticed that she was gone and the game always ended with or without her. It pained her. It still pains her. She tells him how she has always wanted to write, but that her memory is no longer as good as it used to be, and that she has begun to forget everything. He drinks more wine in the hope that it will help him understand what this woman who lives under his bed is saying to him. He wipes away the sweat from his forehead more than once. The smells of alcohol and perspiration drift out of his open mouth and he starts to pant for breath like an amateur horseman. She begins telling him enthusiastically about her other childhood games, for example, her very favourite game: Open This Door for Me.

She stands in the exact centre of a circle made by the children, defenceless and exposed. The children clasp hands and tug at each other with interlaced fingers. The circle contracts and expands in surging waves. In the middle stands the victim. She is the victim, both pathetic and belligerent. She declares war on the joined arms that surround her. In an attempt to break the siege she dashes forward like a sacrificial offering that has torn loose from its tether. Her blood boils and her face grows red, she is like a bull driven to frenzy by the hand of the matador. 'Open this door for me!' The sing-song reply follows: 'The ox has given birth!' The frenzied beast fears that they'll steal her calf away, so better not open the door and let her escape. The arms, joined in a spiralling circle, draw closer and closer around her body. When they grew a little older the words of the chorus changed to 'Open your eyes, flower; close your eyes, flower.' She turns and turns like a bee dropping into the stamen of a flower. She searches for a way out of the circle that represents the delicate petals of a flower devouring its victim. The girls abandon her one by one.

Charlie has grown tired of listening to her. His face has assumed a bored, knowing expression. 'I understand completely. I understand how you feel,' he says to stem the flow of pointless memories. Charlie doesn't realise that loneliness is to blame; a desperate need to connect to just about anybody, even to a person with the face of a frog and a body that gives off the odours of sweat and lust and expediency.

As he climbs the narrow stairway he grabs her hand and starts to pull her up behind him to the room that lies right above her son's head; her son who is probably poring over his map of Africa at that very moment. Charlie's eyes are bloodshot from fatigue and from listening to her endless stories. He pops open a bottle of beer and lights a cigarette, then he pounces on her, his hands creeping over the bare skin exposed by her low-cut dress. She tells him simply that she can't sleep with him because she doesn't love him. She says it as succinctly as possible: 'I don't love you.' She shivers as she says it, like a blood-red sea-crab just emerged from the water. He tries to convince her of the truth that love and hate mean nothing in the dance, as in life, and that all she has to do is relax the muscles of her mind and give her body a chance to express itself, but Hend is unconvinced. The fragile spell cast by the wine and the circle of dancers has been broken and Charlie is once again a clay frog of a man she doesn't love. She knows that he wants her to be like that other woman, the one who left her daughter at Hend's apartment out of the blue one day. She dodges his stifling arms and runs away. She hears him slam the door behind her and mutter expressively: 'Big fat ass.' Exhausted, she cries alone in her room.

At the next dance class she worries more about her big fat ass than her dance steps and she makes even more stupid mistakes, turning round and round in halting circles, desperately trying to imitate the other women. He takes her hand doggedly, as though he were training an obstinate mule: 'One, foot forward, two, together, three, backward . . .' She concentrates on her high-heeled shoes and moves her feet carefully but she still can't get it right. 'Don't look at your feet,' he yells at her. 'Here,' he points to his eyes, 'look here.' She knows what men are like when they get tired of a woman. They get just the way Charlie did when he put his hand around her waist impatiently and twirled her in a lumbering, clumsy circle. Suddenly he stands perfectly still and says in front of everyone, 'I'm not going to eat you. No one in this world intends to eat you, I can promise you that. This is just a dance, my dear.' She pulls away from him and stands alone, staring at her crooked feet in the mirror. But he isn't finished. 'My dear, you have to leave your inhibitions at the door and give your body a chance to express itself.' He says this in the calm and professional tone of a dance instructor, but her face turns red with mortification and her heart begins to thump in her chest. He spends the rest of the lesson focusing on the other middle-aged women as they move about nimbly. Hend decides that dancing is not for her. Neither is love, for that matter, or anything that she had ever set her heart on. After class, she watches him cross the street, jump onto his bike and disappear down Seventh Avenue. She walks back alone through the dark streets that lead to her house.

From then on they carefully avoid each other. Her friend

Fatima, who had also taken a few classes at his studio, has started to pay him visits at home. Hend hears the sound of her perfectly formed rear end going up and down the stairs. She never stops to knock at Hend's door and say hello or tell her what she is doing up there. Only the scent of Hend's clove tea floats up to them in the evening, while the smell of his cigarettes and the rustle of their whispers float down through the window that exposes her little home to the world's indifferent gaze.

7

Atlantic Avenue

The first thing that Americans do when they wake up in the morning is hurry off to Dunkin' Donuts. The Dunkin' Donuts at the corner of Atlantic and Fourth Avenues is a pale salmon colour. The oldest community of Arab-American immigrants lives in the neighbourhood. Next door to the Dunkin' Donuts stands a mosque frequented by African-American Muslims, then there's the Yemeni restaurant called Sabaa, and a number of shops that sell miswak toothpicks and musk oil and Qurans and prayer rugs. There's also a home for the elderly nearby, as well as a homeless shelter, a spa, and a welfare office on Fulton Street where the poor go for food stamps and unemployment benefits. Female workers – especially immigrants – are in high demand because their wages are generally lower, and because employers imagine that women of colour are better at communicating with customers who look like them, customers who can understand their heavy accents and argue comfortably about pennies counted out with vigilance.

She leaves him sleeping deeply. She resents the thought of him waking up in an empty apartment, getting dressed by himself, struggling over his shoelaces. She won't know for sure whether he's wrapped his scarf tight around his neck against the biting cold or whether he'll be safe crossing the street alone and walking to school with no one to watch over him. She panics whenever she sees a poster of a missing child. A sharp needle of grief pricks her heart because she knows he has to grow up and become a man without any help from her. She's afraid for him. She gazes at his round, healthy cheeks and wide black eyes and the broad smile that he bestows upon friends and strangers alike. She is constantly warning him about passers-by and neighbours and strangers and schoolmates older than him, about teachers and classrooms and the school bathrooms and football tackles. She has tried to explain to him that he is a little man already, that he must never let any other man touch him, whether in affection or anger, but she cannot be sure that he has understood her. 'Fine,' he would reply impatiently, and again, in English: '*Fine.*'

But that hasn't eased her fear. She is afraid when she hurries down the street in the dark just before dawn and hops onto an empty bus, and she is afraid when she walks alone from the bus stop to the Dunkin' Donuts in front of which knots of people huddle in the early hours of the morning, trying to force their eyes open with a cup of hot black coffee. She changes her clothes quickly in front of Fatima (who doesn't resemble her in the least). Fatima is much younger than her, a dark-skinned Somali girl in her late twenties, tall and slender. Her body is flawless, not an ounce of flab, no traces of childbirth or abuse, and her kinky African hair is cut close to her head like a beautiful boy's. Fatima is the cashier. She is the exact type of woman that the customers like. She colours her hair white blonde, which creates a sharp contrast with her small, childish features and shining black skin, and gives her face a kind of electric sensuality. Fatima was born to be a leading lady. She stands behind the counter and moves her nimble fingers between the bills and the Styrofoam cups of coffee with a sweet, tranquil smile hovering on her lips. 'Would you like anything else? Do you want it black or with cream and sugar? Skim milk or whole?' Then she would wish you a nice day – sometimes a beautiful day – but sometimes she just smiles that quizzical, tender smile that makes the customer feel like an old and cherished friend. They come back again and again on cold, rainy winter mornings because they are addicted to the radiance of her face. Hend's role unfolds, as usual, behind the scenes. She wipes away the coffee stains and arranges the doughnuts in neat rows and mops the floor quite gracefully – but no one ever notices, of course. She is constantly on the move between toilets and tables, sometimes distracted and absent-minded, other times frowning and pensive.

She spends the whole morning mopping the dirty salmon floor. She stoops slightly as she moves from one table to another. Her rump sticks out, round and strapping, the posterior of a Middle Eastern woman who spends all her time sitting in the same place. Some of the women watch it approvingly as she vigorously attacks the dirty tables. The men are usually drawn to Fatima, no matter what she's doing: frowning, daydreaming, baring her small white teeth in a grin that sets off her full lips. In the morning the workers come, followed by the students. When it starts to rain, the homeless people drift in from all over and greet each other as though they'd made appointments to meet in that very place. They scrupulously count out the round coins in their dirty pockets and then they stand in a long line to order coffee. All day they drag their carts piled high with bric-a-brac:

old clothes and shoes, discarded bits of odds and ends, food and drink and blankets. Their shoes are caked in the mud of the surrounding streets and the air fresheners inside aren't enough to dissipate the powerful odour that comes off their skin in waves. They look at her shyly as though asking permission to sit down in peace for a while until the rain stops, and they sit there in proud silence as they tuck their ragged clothes out of sight under their coats. She passes between them to wipe down the tables. They hide inside the close warmth of the place. Dunkin' Donuts is a twenty-four-hour refuge for them, as it is for foreigners with big dreams that are always just out of reach.

She presses her nose against the window glass and watches the snow cover the streets. She starts thinking about him again. Why does God create mothers? Is he running through the playground now? Will he fall and break something on the slippery ground? Will the other kids make fun of his accent? Has he found someone to talk to, or is he still standing alone with his back to the wall like the other immigrant kids? Has he understood that sticking out your middle finger at someone is an obscene gesture, and that it's meant as a grave insult? Do the other kids give him the finger to test his cultural competence?

She moves away from the window and picks up her mop again. She sprays air freshener in the bathrooms to dissipate the oppressive winter air.

Every morning, Fatima takes her shirt off in front of Hend in the bathroom, where they change into their uniforms. Little red spots cover her back and neck. She scratches her skin ferociously, then gently rubs in layers of ointment before carefully putting on her clothes. Hend asks her about the inflamed pimples. 'Bed-bugs,' she replies in disgust. 'Haven't you heard of them? Don't you know what they are?' She tells Hend that bedbugs live in the folds of your mattress and come out at night to suck your blood. She says that they feed on the blood of their sleeping victims, and that they reproduce a thousand times every night. They're entirely resistant to pesticides and repellents, they burrow into wood and stick to clothes, and the only way to get rid of them is to burn everything. Hend never knows where Fatima sleeps. Sometimes she spends the night at 'John's house', other times, at some other man's place. She doesn't like anyone to ask her about the pimples, or about the men, or about Somalia. She dreams of becoming another Naomi Campbell because Naomi's got a tall, slender, graceful figure that hints of faraway countries, just like her.

They walk next to each other down the streets that the two of them have come to know like the backs of their hands. Sometimes Hend sits alone for a couple of hours on a wooden chair in front of a washing machine owned by one of the religious Yemenis. He always greets her modestly in the Islamic manner – *asalamu 'alaikum* – then turns his face away from Fatima's leotard-clad body. They sit together and puff on the cigarettes that they've been postpon-ing since early morning. Fatima never talks about herself. She isn't like the other immigrants who love to chatter and gossip and in-vent stories to fill up the blank spaces in their lives. Hend knows that Fatima only hangs around with her so that she can spend the night at her place every once in a while when she needs to get away from John or another ex-boyfriend. There isn't much spare room in Hend's studio, so when Fatima sleeps over she has to lay a mattress on the only available floor space in front of the kitchenette. When she is staying with Hend, Fatima races up the many flights of stairs, bursts into the apartment, and immediately heads for the shower. She gives her body up to the pulsing water (maybe it will heal those spots on her back). She spends most of her time showering and rubbing lotions into her skin and watching the world go by from the only window in the apartment. She offers Hend advice about her son as he sits quietly drawing his map of Africa: 'This kid is going to stay stuck to you like that forever. You should leave him to me – I'll take care of him.' She plays chess with him sometimes – a game the boy has discovered a talent for.

Fatima is even more beautiful than Naomi Campbell but nobody seems to want to discover her. Maybe this is why she wraps herself tightly in the blanket at night, covers her face in the same way Hend does, and tosses and turns endlessly: another solitary, pitiful woman in the apartment. Hend draws a little comfort from the likeness. She too likes to press up against windows and dream. At first Hend believed that Fatima was her friend and that she came over to keep her company. Now she realises that she is just looking for a free ride, that she isn't a friend after all, and this makes Hend feel even lonelier. A friend is someone who freely gives sympathy and understanding, and this is exactly what Fatima is unable to give. She is too preoccupied with her pimples and her skin and her obscure future.

Hend lives in a world of her own too. She often thinks about her old friends and realises that they have been few and far between. She has never been very sociable or vivacious and amusing. She ascribes this to her timid, introverted birth sign. Nobody could penetrate the tough outer skin that she hides beneath. At school she sat between Noha and Hanan; Noha on her right and Hanan on her left. Noha's woman-body blossomed quickly but she still liked to play with Hend. Her favourite game of all was hopscotch and she was always playing it on the sidewalk in front of her father's shop. When her dress flew up as she jumped from square to square, Hend could see the inflamed spoon marks on her thighs. Noha loved hopscotch. She would carefully draw the squares with a piece of chalk, pull up her dress, fling out her shapely white legs and relentlessly pursue the pebble as it skipped from square to square with astonishing speed. A group of boys from the Muqawi School always stopped to stare at her bare legs as they passed by, and she would pull up her dress even further, not caring one bit about the consequences. Keeping her legs raised high for as long as possible was the first womanly skill that Noha had acquired and her talent began to capture the attention of passers-by who would stop to watch her skipping from square to square in wonder. Then her furious mother would pull her away by the hair and drag her inside.

Their house was made up of two rooms behind the small shop owned by Noha's father, Amm Mahmud the grocer. Noha watched as her mother took off her dress and a plump woman called Fatma al-Qarumiya proceeded to rub her tired back with a paste made of olive oil and plaster. Fleshy, dark-skinned Fatma al-Qarumiya massaged her back as she sat on a rush mat in the airless room. Her hand slid down from the top of her spinal cord to the compact base of her torso while Noha eavesdropped on the advice she gave her mother as she relaxed into the massage. 'So what, seven girls? Your oldest is a boy – what more does he want from you? Another boy? Humph. That's all he needs! How on earth is Mahmud the grocer going to support all those male-kids he's constantly dreaming about having?'

Noha's mother slapped her cheek pitifully. 'But he says he's going to get married, Auntie!'

Fatma al-Qarumiya grabbed hold of the woman's naked legs. 'Listen to me . . . raise your legs.' She depilated the triangle between her thighs with caramelised sugar, then rubbed some oil into it. When she had finished, she sagely nodded her head, which was decorated with two bird tattoos like the ones the gypsies have. 'All men are sons of bitches, you silly woman. They're like dogs, hanging on to the world by their cocks.' She said this with the wisdom of a woman who had known all kinds of men in her long life; a woman who had achieved complete harmony with the ways of the world.

Noha's mother's skin was loose and drooping from all those pregnancies and her stomach was bloated with layers of fat and criss-crossed with long stretch marks. Fatma al-Qarumiya slapped the woman's stomach. 'Suck that in,' she said. Then she pointed to her legs. 'Raise those up.' She poured a mixture of oil and warm, perfumed water onto them and the dusty ground greedily sucked up the sweet mastic. Noha's mother put on a transparent, open-necked slip printed with pink flowers and decorated with a ribbon around the collar. She smiled, plump and fragrant and ready for the night ahead.

The mother caught her daughter spying on her from behind

the half-open door and she pounced on her, pulling her by the hair and pinching her thighs with all the force of her pent-up frustrations. 'All day long she plays hopscotch and spreads her legs wide, Auntie. The girl is going to bring calamity down upon me. I've told her over and over, "Don't you dare spread those legs of yours, girl!"' Noha cried as she told Hend about it, but she kept on playing hopscotch in the school yard because she knew that the game brought out all her hidden talents. She drew the squares and spread her legs and skipped ever so gracefully from square to square, and she didn't give a damn that the boys were spying on her. She balanced the pebble on her head, then tossed it with her eyes closed and skipped away to escape the fate that awaited her mother after the massage of oil and mastic: that moment when she would emerge from the bedroom with wild, unkempt hair and red bruises on her cheeks.

The voice of Noha's father, Amm Mahmud the grocer, would follow her — but it was not the gentle and tolerant voice that he used to bargain with his customers. As he shouted at his wife, it sounded like a fierce, drawn-out hiss. 'What are you, a piece of rock, you bitch?' Noha's mother would cry and complain of a splitting headache that never left her, and Fatma al-Qarumiya treated it by engraving a tattoo right where it was tender. Noha, meanwhile, balanced the pebble on her head and tried to forget what her mother's face looked like as she gathered in her seven daughters on the mat around her and painfully hunched over them like an old rag. Still, she was always ready for her husband because she never knew when he might want her. He shook her by the shoulder some nights and said, 'Come.'

Noha practised more and played even harder, so hard that Hend was reduced to watching her friend zip around the court alone, never ever falling or stumbling. Meanwhile, Amm Mahmud the grocer sat in his shop behind the wooden counter that was covered by a filthy stone slab they called 'the bank'. The women parked their breasts there or plopped down their nursing infants on it as they negotiated with him over the exact number of pennies in their pockets. Sometimes they even came out of these negotiations with a free handful of dried mint or a thin slice of the spun sugar or sesame halva that sat uncovered in the window. The grocer sold cigarettes too, but tobacco wasn't the only thing he rolled into them. 'Satlana' – that which intoxicates the mind – was the other ingredient. 'Stuffed or plain?' he asked his customers. The bottles of soda and Stella beer, the barrels of oil and ghee and the sacks of sugar paled in importance compared with the rolling paper and the hashish cigarettes that were his most profitable source of income. Those townspeople who had grown rich from the suitcases and money orders coming from Iraq and Yemen and Saudi Arabia were his most valued customers. With the money he made from this trade he built a couple of brick rooms behind his shop and installed an iron gate to prevent his seven daughters from spilling out onto the streets.

Hend would stand on the other side of that gate, trying but usually failing to catch a glimpse of her friend. Noha's mother was more often than not the only person in sight. She would sit just behind the gate, pulling in the smoke from the water pipe and breathing it out through her nostrils. A fish tattoo decorated her temple and a necklace of plastic fish hung round her neck along with a few chilli peppers: charms against the evil eye that she took to wearing after moving into her new red-brick house. And while it was true that God had blessed them with money, He had cursed her – Umm Noha – with headaches and migraines.

Mahmud the grocer eventually built a second floor made up of two rooms with a stone staircase. He was the first one in town to add another floor to his house, and he painted the upper rooms pink. He began to spread the word of his matrimonial intentions amongst all the women who leaned up against his 'bank': 'I want to get officially married – I swear! The Prophet came to me in a dream and said, "Mahmud, at least God gave you one son – I only begat girls." So I said, "Bless you, I just want another little boy to carry the load," and he replied, "It's your God-given right, Mahmud."'

And so Mahmud the grocer married a young, skinny girl in the hope that her back would be stronger and her womb more hospitable than his first wife's, and that therefore she would be more likely 'to bring the boy to term', as Fatma al-Qarumiya – who knew all about women – advised him. She pulled on the hashish cigarette that he gave her and said cheerfully, 'Brother, God said marry two women or three women. I know the well and its cover like the back of my hand. The mother of your children is finished – not an ounce of suppleness or beauty left in her.' Noha's mother's migraines grew worse, and Noha started to tell Hend all kinds of stories about her newborn siblings. One day Noha's father said to her, 'I'll kill you if you ever play hopscotch again. Do you want to bring scandal down on us, girl?' So Noha began collecting shards of pottery for her new game.

Hopscotch – that perilous, obscene game – was replaced by the game of beads. Noha took Hend by the hand and ran off to the pottery workshop behind the Hill Estate. Inside the workshop there were mounds of raw clay and finished crockery and round, smooth, long-necked water jars in red and white, turned on an iron lathe to produce the perfect, narrow holes that neatly disbursed their liquid into the drinker's mouth. The pitchers, unlike the water jars, had large, projecting spouts that shamelessly disgorged their water onto the bare thighs of people washing out in the open. There were other things for sale in the workshop: oven paddles; huge storage jars for water, standing there erect and virile; puffed-up clay jars like pregnant bellies; dovecotes for pigeon chicks to sleep in. The way of the world: forms whimsically created by the master craftsman, then burned in the fiery kiln and laid out on the straw facing the workshop for the passing women to pick up and examine, and perhaps even buy.

Hend and Noha ran off together and climbed Pharaoh's Hills. In order to reach the pottery workshop they had to cross the open space where the Friday market was held and pass the gypsy camp. They tirelessly collected bits of broken pottery and ran back home with their booty. They sat on the doorstep of Amm Mahmud's shop and proceeded to round the broken shards into smooth beads that they scooped up and tossed with long, experienced fingers as their plastic bracelets jingled merrily on their wrists. But once again Noha's angry mother came out to drag her daughter away by the hair and pinch her thighs because 'the girl has gotten into the habit of wandering around like a stray cat'. And that was the last time Hend and Noha ever played together.

She spied on Amm Mahmud's shop in the hope that she would catch a glimpse of her friend making paper cones for the sugar or polishing the slippery floor. Now she only ever saw her sitting behind the iron gate and playing beads alone, every movement executed with a grace and skill that only Noha could possess – the grace and skill of someone who was used to playing alone. When Hend asked about her friend, Noha's mother said: 'That's it, no more schooling for her.' But that didn't stop Hend from hanging around the iron gate that no one ever opened for her. Her old friend talked to her from the other side with the calmness and self-possession of a little woman. The sculptor of girls visited her before any of the other girls. Her face grew fuller and her body more lithe, and she walked now with a deliberate, self-conscious stride. Hend watched her behind the gate as she played alone, surrounded by the odour of kerosene coming from the corrugated-iron barrels and by plastic containers of oil and canvas sacks of sugar. Noha never came out, and a few months later she disappeared entirely while Fatima al-Qarumiya came and went through the iron gate with her kit of pastes and oils and medicines for nausea and pregnancy, and when Hend asked her about Noha, Fatma laughed that deep, masculine laugh of hers that terrified children and excited the lust of passing men, and said, 'The sculptor of girls kidnapped her.'

✻

Hend's other friend, Hanan, was round and heavy with skin the colour of wheat, a miniature version of her mother, The Lady Umm Hanan the seamstress. Once Noha had gone to live with the sculptor of girls, Hanan and Hend would sit next to each other on the sofa of her mother's house and Hanan would show her the colourful snippets of leftover fabric that she hid in her pockets and used to make blackboard erasers or soft cotton rags for wiping the chalk off your fingers. Hanan was always wiping the board clean and the whole classroom would stare at her round, plump rear end as she did it. Hanan didn't know how to play hopscotch, or beads either, but she was very good at making rag dolls and blackboard wipes. She was also good at cutting out patterns for doll dresses, especially ones with lots of frills – all from the leftover fabric that she gathered from under her mother's sewing machine. She embroidered the dresses with sequins and coloured stones and sold them to the girls in the other classes for five milliemes apiece. She drew eyebrows and mouths on her rag dolls with coloured pens and sewed two green stones in for eyes. In arts and crafts class she crocheted tablecloths with the duck stitch like a practised housewife. She also sold crocheted hats that she made herself, as well as scarves and embroidered handkerchiefs. Her passion for embroidery and her quiet perseverance were extraordinary, and she became an expert at making exquisite tablecloths that she called 'sunflowers' because they were the colour of open sunflowers in all their glorious shades from dark brown to bright sunshine yellow.

The only game that Hanan was good at was Little House. She would come to Hend's house and collect the empty matchboxes from the garbage, as well as old bottles and cartons. Together they traced out the borders of their imaginary house in the sand with pebbles and scraps and some tree branches and leaves. Everything was now ready to play-act mother and daughter. Hanan was the daughter and called Hend 'Mama', or sometimes she was the maid and called her 'ma'am'. She was anything Hend wanted her to be, because Hanan had been trained to obey. She was sedate and well behaved, an immovable object, while Hend ran around like a lunatic in the courtyard that hosted an imaginary house of dust full of imaginary stoves and refrigerators and beds.

Sometimes Hend's mother sent her to Umm Hanan's house with clothes that needed altering. Hanan's mother took them in or let them out or shortened them, from one child to the next. Hend skipped happily through the narrow streets covered in straw. Women sat at their doorsteps, washing the dishes and drinking tea or exchanging good-natured insults. Hend liked Umm Hanan's house because it was always full of women, the door always stood wide open, and the hubbub of the sewing machine and the transistor radio gave it a festive atmosphere quite different from that of her own home. Umm Hanan was stout and dark-skinned. Her voice was mellow and pleasant to the ear and she liked to sing. They called her Fathiya Ahmad – after the actress – because she had thin eyebrows that she painted with kohl. Her eyes were deep black, she wore her hair in a chignon perched coquettishly at the side of her head, and she always matched the colour of her hat to her outfit. Her voice sent shivers down Hend's spine, especially when she bent over her machine and sang that particular song: 'If Only We Could Be Together Again'. She also sang songs to make the girls laugh. She wiggled her eyebrows wickedly as she sang: 'Pull the Curtain Against the Breeze Before the Neighbours Break Our Hearts'.

Umm Hanan's breasts were full under the frill of her plunging neckline, but there was still enough room for the scissors and the sewing needle and other little items like her tweezers and eyebrow pencil and her change purse. Her round breasts could still be compared to all the usual fruits because she never breastfed any of her three daughters, but gave them to her sister to nurse instead. When she bent over her sewing machine her breasts spilled out over the frills of her dress.

Her house was full of young girls who had come to learn the trade. They called her 'ma'am' and Hend never saw them sitting at the machine. Mostly they swept and cooked and scattered water in the street in front of the house to tamp down the dust, but when Umm Hanan began to cut out a piece of fabric they huddled around her on the rush mat and tried to memorise her every move. Umm Hanan's mother lived with her. She was an extremely thin old lady with lots of wrinkles. She liked to sit in the sun because it soothed her inflamed eyes, crusted and shut fast with ophthalmia. She quietly peeled the garlic or shelled the peas, breaking her silence only to do her ablutions and pray for the Prophet or tell a few stories to the girls now and then. They had to repeat everything they said to her because she was hard of hearing. Hend knew that she used to bake bread in people's houses like Grandmother Zaynab, but then she retired when the pain in her eyes got worse thanks to the heat and smoke of the ovens. One day Hend came by with a message. 'Mama says can you make some pies for her for Ramadan, Grandmother?' Umm Hanan got up in a huff from her spot at the sewing machine. 'Tell Mama that we don't work for the Bedouins any more,' she said emphatically as she wiggled her eyebrows, 'and my mother doesn't make pies or bread any more either.' Hend remembers feeling mortified. She didn't understand who these 'Bedouins' were in the first place, or what her family had to do with them.

Umm Hanan played with the radio dial every few hours to find her favourite songs. At some point, she started to refuse the mending work that Hend brought from her mother. 'Tell your mother that I don't do alterations any more,' she said bluntly. 'My scissors only cut brand-new clothes now.' Hend stared at the floor self-consciously as she stood there with the old clothes in her hand. Umm Hanan must have felt sorry for her because she took them gently and said, 'Alright then, just this once for Mama's sake. But tell her that my scissors are legendary and that she'll never see anything like the cut of my sleeves.' Hend nodded her head obediently and went to sit next to the old grandmother, who told her the story of 'Hend the daughter of King Nu'man'. She watched the girls as they scrubbed the pots and pans. They stole glances at Umm Hanan as she yawned and said, 'My back is killing me, girls. One of you can fix this piece.' She left the machine to them and stretched out on her stomach on the rush mat. She nodded off as one of the girls massaged her back. Sometimes they plucked stray hairs from her eyebrows or her plump legs without being asked, as if they'd been trained from the start to do that kind of thing. Umm Hanan emerged from these sessions glowing and smooth-skinned, looking just like Fathiya Ahmad, especially when the kohl smudged in circles under her eyes. Her men friends were in the habit of dropping by the house. They walked in as though they owned the place, stretching out comfortably in the living room with its three clean, brightly coloured sofas. Umm Hanan's door was never shut fast, and anyone outside could easily hear her echoing laugh and the sound of her fine, plaintive voice as she sang.

One day the two girls went up to the roof, Hanan pulling Hend by the hand. They climbed the wooden ladder and lay down together on the straw. Hanan wept, and her voice sounded exactly like her mother's. 'She wants to get married. Every day she tells me the same thing. "I don't know where your father is. From the day he left for Jordan he hasn't sent a word or a penny. He said he'd be back in the blink of an eye but he never came. I'm not going to stay single like this forever, living without a man, and you're older now and you've got to understand."'

Hanan's mother didn't get married after all, but certainly not for lack of suitors. Hanan grew up and sprouted full breasts and rounded buttocks before any of the other girls. This provoked the Arabic teacher and he would make her wipe the blackboard on purpose so that he could examine the telltale signs of her approaching womanhood at his leisure. He talked a lot about the ancient Bedouins' passion for female posteriors. Hanan disappeared from class suddenly, like Noha, and when Hend took a bag of oranges and went to visit her, ill with a stomach ache at home, Umm Hanan laughed coquettishly and purred, 'That's it . . . your little friend is a woman now.' Hend sat next to Hanan and Hanan told her about the talcum powder and her aching legs and the cramps. Hend thought long and hard about the sculptor of girls and wondered why he still hadn't paid her a visit, she alone amongst all the girls. She waited impatiently for him to come and take her as far away as possible.

Soon, different kinds of guests started to come to Umm Hanan's house. Some of them wore the white Bedouin headdress. They looked a lot like Hend's uncles, impassive under the weight of their heavy robes. A few months later, one of them carried Hanan off to his distant country, a place further away even than the Red Estate, or Jordan, or anywhere Hend had ever heard of. Umm Hanan abandoned her sewing machine and built two new rooms out of red brick. She began to shut her door fast from then on, a new door made of elaborately carved wood. The townswomen would come to examine her merchandise: Saudi gowns and Gulf-style scarves, black veils and heavy stockings for covered women. She changed her title from The Lady Umm Hanan to The Hajja Umm Hanan. She took to visiting the blessed city of Medina and the Prophet's tomb every few months and she'd come back carrying suitcases full of merchandise. She would sell and bargain and swear on the Blessed Prophet's tomb that she had 'loved' it (meaning that she had kissed it) with her own two lips. She insisted that she never made any profit, and that she only did it for the love of God. She also began to praise the virtue of the town's young women to the skies and she offered to marry them off in those pure and blessed faraway countries, free of charge, her only recompense being the approval of the Creator of All Things, and the joy of settling the girls – especially the youngest of them – comfortably in life. The neighbours started to place all their hopes in her and her business. They sent the spinsters to work as servants and married off the youngest and prettiest of their daughters in distant Saudi Arabia. They began to say that her visits were blessed, especially when she knocked on their doors in her elaborately embroidered velvet gown and repeated any one of her newly acquired expressions: 'May God reward you with good' or 'May God permit me to do a good deed with every step' or 'In God's keeping' – those turns of phrase that clothed her in an aura of strength and purpose.

Hend sat alone in her classroom at the Muqawi School. She was the only girl left in the class now that all the other girls had disappeared, one after the other. She sat there, quiet and well behaved, convinced that hopscotch was a shameful game that made girls spread their legs and that beads were sinful because they disturbed the peace of households and brought about their ruin. She even began to hate Little House because houses were places that thrived on wretchedness and calamity. After Hanan disappeared, she didn't want to have friends any more, or maybe she just didn't know how to make them. She started to refer to the people she met as 'classmates' or 'acquaintances'.

Here in Brooklyn, she waits for the phone to ring or for a strange woman to smile at her on the street. She doesn't see Fatima any more either. 'Everybody in this city is running around after something. Everybody is busy,' she would say to make herself feel better. She walks alone towards Atlantic Avenue. The winter rain falls steadily and the homeless people hide in the subway station or make a quick dash for Dunkin' Donuts. They sit alone and glance longingly at strangers with whom they hope to exchange a smile or a few simple words. The rain falls on the glass windows of the coffee shop and she watches the solitary drops and thinks how closely she fits in with the wretchedness around her. As she walks down the long avenue she passes the halal butchers and the stores that sell fragrant oils and religious books about the torments of hell, pilgrimage clothes and velvet Meccan prayer rugs and short white Pakistani jalabas and so many different kinds of headscarves. Sometimes she rides the bus from Atlantic Avenue in the north of Brooklyn to Coney Island or Brighton Beach in the south. She sits next to the window and remembers how she used to love watching the world go by from the window of the old Cadillac. She stays on the bus till the end of the line and then rides back again, without getting off.

She sits down on the wooden bench near his school. The boy she's waiting for has grown taller somehow. He walks a few steps ahead of her in silence. He answers her questions abruptly, '*Fine,*' and then he suddenly says this: 'Life is hard here. But you have to keep dreaming because dreams do come true sometimes.' She has no idea where he got that from, but she tells him that she likes the way he pronounces the words in English. '*Dreams come true sometimes, Mom.*'

8

Fulton Street

Fulton Street runs through the heart of Brooklyn. A small one-storey building with a back garden and terrace stands on a small side street opposite a church. They call it the Refugee Assistance Agency. She goes there every week and takes her place next to the young women, and older ones like herself, who come here looking for work and food stamps or a meagre weekly handout. The women are from Burma and Bosnia, Iraqi women in cheerless black robes, fair-skinned Kurdish women, and Afghans with bright, flushed faces.

Hend always sits next to Nazahat. Nazahat, who fled Bosnia years ago, has a habit of producing an ID card from her pocket every so often to prove that she used to be a doctor back home in a city that Hend has never heard of. Her face is small and pink and she wears thick prescription glasses that give her a dignified look. Her voice is measured and grave – as a doctor's voice should be – and her limited English is Russian-accented. Thanks to her many skills, Nazahat is much sought after by immigrants with no health insurance from the communities scattered on the peripheries of Brooklyn and particularly in the area of Canarsie. The Refugee Assistance Agency is usually full of them: legal and illegal immigrants, many from conservative Yemeni Muslim families who all live together in big houses. Nazahat's skills open the door to their world. She is an expert at diagnosing and treating all kinds of aches and pains. She takes her patients' pulses and checks their blood pressure and temperature. She examines pregnant and nursing women, and the families always send for her in emergencies. They call her 'doctor' and they trust her because she is a Muslim, and therefore permitted to examine the private parts of other Muslims. She also carries a small portable sewing machine with her as she goes from home to home so that she can alter the voluminous black abayas at the waist or neckline or hips; shapeless clothing that has been transported to New York in standard sizes by merchants and returning pilgrims.

Nazahat's hands are accomplished hands, small and agile and criss-crossed with minute veins, the hands of a miracle worker. The only Arabic phrases she understands are 'God willing', 'thank God', 'take it out here', 'take it in there', and a few other basic expressions that she needs to communicate with her clients – especially with the old matriarch who runs all those households from her permanent spot on the prayer rug, where she constantly murmurs to her beads, 'There is no power or mercy save in God.' The young ones don't resemble their mothers at all. They wear designer clothes and speak fluent American English in spite of the fact that they rarely make it past junior high school because the grandmother promptly arranges early marriages for them from her spot on the prayer rug. Nazahat's services are especially in demand during the marriage season. She is the one who cuts and sews trousseaux and prepares facials and treats pelvic inflammations and prescribes ointments of various kinds. She plays the roles of bathhouse attendant and nurse all wrapped up in one. The matriarch, who chews on mouthfuls of qat grown in the small garden behind the house and rubs her hands with saffron and aloe musk, is fond of her, and calls her 'a true Muslim'. Nazahat also does the shopping for her Yemeni clients because they don't like to send their women to the supermarket. The women mostly take care of the housework and don't go out at all except in the company of their husbands. Hend has discovered that many of these wealthy Yemeni families own most of the delis in Brooklyn as well as a good number of the Brooklyn Laundry Clean franchise stores, and that they compete with the Mexicans in the construction business. They started out as small contractors, then expanded into business dynasties, marrying amongst themselves and forming a 'ghetto' that stretches from Canarsie to Fifth Avenue.

Nazahat sits on her chair in the waiting room of the Refugee Assistance Agency between Hend and a group of young Bosnian women covered from head to foot, and she tells Hend about Omar Azzam. She says that he is very rich and very generous and that he supports dozens of Muslim families with monthly stipends. She urges Hend to meet his wife, Erica, an American girl who saw the light and converted to Islam thanks to him, and who is very charitable to the Muslim refugees in Brooklyn. Omar Azzam is rich – richer than anyone could imagine, richer even than his Yemeni partners in the construction and deli businesses. Hend turns her face to the window to escape the conversation. 'That kind of charity isn't for me,' she says. 'I don't have anything to do with the God that you people are always talking about. Or at least I'm trying to forget Him for now.' Nazahat turns her back on Hend and doesn't say another word.

The group of women who sit to the side at a distance from the circle of men are plump like her. Their rear ends are heavy and they use obscure body language to reply to simple questions like 'How are you?' There is something slightly bizarre about them. Their transparent Uzbek scarves partially conceal their faces, and they wear strange dresses printed with primitive shapes – squares and triangles – in bright colours, red and green like the flags of disappeared nations drowned in some unknown sea. They smile for no reason. Their children will grow up and learn to speak American English and they will never ask after their absent fathers. Their papers are marked 'physical and emotional abuse . . . humanitarian asylum' – phrases that Hend understands too well. A large group of relatively young men also wait at the agency. Most of them are from Burma or Afghanistan and they exchange a few listless words until their turn comes to receive their handouts. They don't talk much because each of them is preoccupied with his own affairs. They don't share their stories like the women do because they want to forget them. They look forward to becoming ordinary American citizens in a few years and never again having to answer the question, 'Where do you come from?'

✽

Abdul approaches her with a big smile on his face. She has seen him around before. He is twenty years younger than her and desperate to find a job and a woman to keep him company. She smiles back but she doesn't want to get involved in a conversation because he talks too much and isn't very intelligent. He asks her the same question that he asks everyone, just to pass the time.

'Are you from the agency?'

She shakes her head.

'Arab?'

She nods.

'Iraqi?'

She shakes her head.

'Ah. Palestinian, right?'

She shakes her head. 'I'm Egyptian,' she answers curtly, hoping to nip the conversation in the bud.

'Christian, right?'

She doesn't reply. She withdraws into herself even more, but Abdul isn't giving up.

'Do you go to the English class?'

She nods.

'And the job-training classes?'

She shakes her head no. Her head is getting tired from all this shaking, but he still won't shut up. He wants to show off, to prove to her that he is some kind of expert on refugee affairs. He tells her that he is from Afghanistan, and she thinks how his small brown eyes are like the eyes of a mountain wolf. He volunteers his story, a pack of lies like everyone else's in this place. They lie to cover up things that they don't want anyone to know and they bury the truth deep down, deeper than anybody could see. He tells her that he used to work for the American army, and he says it proudly.

Abdul goes out to the terrace to smoke. She follows him because she wants to bum a cigarette, to exhale her anxiety along with the smoke, to get away from the crowd. The agency office is part of the library, just a small room looking out onto Park Avenue. The terrace is full of wooden chairs too. He sits on one of them and crosses his legs. The sun glances off his coal-black hair and lights up his athletic, martial build. He hands her a cigarette as he leans back in his chair against the railing. She sits on the other side of the terrace and smokes in silence.

Abdul grins because he has finally found someone to talk to. 'Do you pray?'

She shakes her head no. She refuses words, words are meaningless. Only silent gestures can guarantee an existence free of lies.

'Do you like vodka?' he asks lewdly. Hend thinks that he must be mocking her loneliness because he asks the question as though he is making her a generous offer. He says it with the cunning of a restless wolf looking for a partner to howl at the moon with. She laughs because she hadn't expected that he would try to seduce her.

'I like vodka, but I don't go out with children,' she replies playfully. Then she looks him straight in the eye and tells him that she prefers to drink alone because when she gets drunk she always cries a lot and then passes out. She adds that men don't usually like to witness this disappointing little drama. He nods his head shrewdly this time, evidently convinced of the wisdom of her observation, and returns to a more general line of questioning.

'Are there American military bases in Egypt? Did you ever work at any of them?' She doesn't respond to this, and he continues: 'I used to translate for the Americans.' He laughs and stubs out his cigarette with his shoe. 'I translated for them, I brought them information and hashish and other stuff. We used to drink Russian vodka and smoke the best Afghan hash together.' He reaches out to touch her hair. 'Do you like Afghan hashish?'

She laughs in spite of herself because he is even more of a child than she thought at first. She imagines that he wishes he could just burst into tears, that he is terribly homesick because he still hasn't found the paradise that he has desperately been looking for. Hend has smoked hash just once in her life, but she doesn't tell him this. She only did it because all she wanted to do was write, so much so that she felt she would die if the bitter mountain of words stayed trapped inside her. She had to finish her first and only manuscript, 'I Am Like No Other', but writing is intractable, like a wounded woman, and at some point she realised that, after all was said and done, she was incapable of healing those wounds. She cried all the time and she desperately searched in every corner for that little girl who used to live inside her. She wanted to burrow deep inside the cocoon of her fears, and that's why she tried smoking the pungent, sticky drug just once, so that she could pick up the pen and set it to paper again. But she still couldn't write. She vomited, then she slept for a long time, and when she woke she found that her son, who was still crawling back then, had thrown his tiny body over her face. 'Mama, Mamaaa!' he bawled. He was hungry and wet from head to foot and the acrid smell of his urine burned her nostrils.

She doesn't tell Abdul any of this because she knows he won't understand. He, meanwhile, is making a superhuman effort to discover the effects of his manly powers on her. 'Afghani hash is moist and soft,' he whispers suggestively, tracing a circle in the shape of a woman's backside with his hands. She ignores him.

The smell of hashish drifts from Abdul's cigarette and it immediately reminds her of her old Arabic teacher. She used to worship her Arabic teachers for some mysterious reason. Maybe it had something to do with the smell of hashish that clung to their clothes, or their poise and style. They seemed to her to exude a kind of masculine magic. This Arabic teacher was always staring at her friend Hanan's breasts, exactly at her breasts, two small, round, lovely protrusions that got bigger by the day. The man was tenacious and inscrutable and he would often reel off difficult and dazzling tongue twisters and make Hanan repeat them quickly, just for fun. Hanan always laughed out loud at the mistakes she made. Her small breasts would shake in hilarity, and this pleased him no end. The Arabic teacher was a very distinguished man, although everyone knew that he was the only son of Grandmother Zaynab, who insisted she wasn't a servant even if she worked in people's houses. She did it because 'her hand was blessed when it came to cooking and baking and crushing the wheat or milking the cows'. Of course, this was the same hand that had raised a man whose shirts were always clean and elegant and whose coal-black, fragrant hair was always meticulously groomed. He was – as the whole school knew – a serious and respectable man, addicted to the cigarettes that Mahmud the grocer sold and particularly fond of Hanan and her mother the seamstress. People often saw him coming and going from Umm Hanan's house and she had been heard serenading him with the popular song 'So What if He's Dark-Skinned, It's the Secret of His Beauty'. He leaned on the table at which Hanan and her mother sat and grinned at the girl. Her plump cheeks flushed pink, a carbon copy of her mother.

He had first noticed this resemblance when his class was suddenly emptied of girls and he started to miss their intoxicating perfume. More than once Mr Emile the principal had come into the classroom to warn him, 'You're going to bring catastrophe down on our heads, man!' But he was too busy observing Hanan's miraculous transformation from a child into a woman to pay any attention to the worried schoolmaster. As for Hend, he was mostly interested in her literary skills. She was now able to read and correct the other students' exercises and write their names on the board and even conduct part of the lesson as he lounged on his chair at the front of the class and exchanged innocent pleasantries with his favourite student.

At the same time that Umm Hanan was borrowing the talcum powder from the neighbours in an attempt to ascertain the onslaught of her daughter's early puberty, the Arabic teacher was busy sending Hanan letters warning her that she would be expelled from school if she didn't come back. Neither Hanan nor her mother bothered to read these letters and Hanan stayed put at home. The Arabic teacher, anxious and distracted, was now obliged to focus his attention on Hend, who realised that she would have to face him alone. She explained the rules of grammar and rhetoric to her classmates while he emptied cigarettes with the cartridge of his pen and stuffed them again with hashish. He started to carry a thin cane around and would get angry for no reason and shout insults ('you cattle!') at his students because, as he said, they came to school without cleaning the dung off their plastic shoes and never washed their rough hands, stained green from cutting clover in the fields. Most of Hend's classmates generally considered school to be a kind of rest period or napping time from their heavy work in the fields and they sat in class with stupid expressions on their faces and fought amongst each other rancorously – which only proved the teacher's point. He took to beating them with his cane. He would stretch them out over his chair and give the backs of their legs a good thrashing. The children would get down off the chair, their mouths set in stony silence, trying to hold back their tears. When he finally got tired of giving out beatings he produced his rolling papers and prepared the tobacco-and-hash mixture while throwing out casual remarks about how cattle never get tired of a good whipping.

Meanwhile, Hend continued to read the lessons out loud in class. Once, when she said to him, 'I'm tired, can't someone else do it?' he yanked her brown school apron and said in that high-pitched voice of his that terrified her, 'Who do you think you are? A king's daughter? Go on and run back to your papa's house. The girl thinks she's a princess! You Bedouins can go to hell.' Hend ran out of the classroom and Mr Emile the principal ran after her, but she didn't stop. She left the Muqawi Primary School behind and walked past the threshing machine and the agricultural cooperative all the way home. From that day on her stomach began to hurt her every time she saw the Arabic teacher. He never called on her in class again and she just sat there staring at the wall and waiting patiently for the interminable lesson to end. Then the Arabic teacher began to wear a white cap and pray a lot. He even started taking the boys to the school mosque to pray as a group every Friday. A few months later he took the boat to a faraway country called Yemen. He wasn't the only one. In those days, a lot of teachers packed their bags and went there.

Grandmother Zaynab wept copious tears and said, 'Son of a bitch, that son of my womb. Son of a bitch, just like his father. He didn't even say, "Mother, I'm leaving." He didn't say goodbye to the mother who slaved over him all his life. Never mind, I hope God goes easy on him and puts the wind in his sails with the sea beneath him and his ships full to the brim.' God seemed to have answered Grandmother Zaynab's prayers, just as He seemed to have blessed her hands. The teacher came back from Yemen with a prayer mark on his forehead, a handful of Meccan musk in his pocket, and a pure white jilbab. He began to spend all his time in the Nur Mosque. He preached to the people and led the Friday prayers and called out from the minaret. The congregation would listen intently to his loud voice as he said things like, 'Oh Prophet of God, your people are overrun by wolves,' and his words brought tears to their eyes. He became famous for his eloquence and zeal. He opened a store selling plastic household goods, the first of its kind in town. He called it 'Al-Baraka'. Then he opened a ceramics and tile shop to cater to the owners of all the new brick houses that were springing up in town. He called it 'Al-Quds'. Then he opened a number of franchises specialising in electrical products and called them 'Al-Furqan'. Pharaoh's Hills had become a different place by then, and Hend would often grow disoriented as she led her father on their walks from the reception house to the Heights.

Abdul playfully tugs on a strand of her hair, bringing her back to him from the maze of her memories. A feeling of anger and humiliation washes over her. She tells him sharply that she doesn't like hashish, or children who play at being grown-ups, or translators and spies – that, in fact, she doesn't like anything about him. She tells him that she doesn't believe in anything any more and that as far as she is concerned, he, Abdul, is nothing but a stupid kid.

Abdul just laughs at this harangue and asks her with the cunning of a mountain wolf, 'So you're the ambassadress of good intentions. They're giving you legal residency and food stamps and sympathy for free. Or maybe you're the ghost of Mother Teresa come from the high seas to strike the fear of God into me . . .'

Abdul's comment hurts her. He doesn't understand why she is here – not that she does, either. It hurts her because she knows that she is more decent and principled than that. He just doesn't understand. She turns her back on him, and he adds a parting shot: 'And on top of everything you have a big ass, and I don't like women whose rear ends are as big as Mount Sinai.'

He laughs at his own joke, pleased to show off his command of American slang and his ability to humiliate people coldly, with a smile and not a trace of anger. She pictures him as a mountain-wolf cub raised at the teat of an American commando unit, an expert on vodka and hashish and blasphemy, with nothing better to do than to taunt a solitary and wretched woman like herself.

9

Pluto in Capricorn

Slow, persistent, and cautious. Winterish and loves routine. Idealistic and ambitious. Conservative; prepared to scale mountains to attain his goals. Kind, ethical, and noble. A careful and tireless striver, like all Capricorn men who know how to plan each step calmly, with confidence and great patience, but who jealously hide their disappointment in failure. They meet adversity with stubborn and solitary persistence, bouncing back and starting all over again. The description fit him perfectly, her friend who died.

The winter rain pounded the windows of Cairo's downtown shops as Hend sat next to her friend in the Tak'iba Café. They always went to the same cafés together. Her friend knew all the waiters by name. He exchanged greetings with them, asked them how they were doing, and which villages they came from. They sat by the window and watched the rivulets of water streaming down the sidewalks. The glass reflected his tense face as he asked her the same old questions; questions she'd grown tired of.

'How's life?'

'Well, it's over now.'

'You've still got a lot ahead of you. You're not going to die.'

He reminded her of her son when he said things like that. She replied with the same listless, resigned tone. 'Where will I go in the end?'

'I don't know.' He frowned. 'I wish we all knew where we'll end up. Things would be much easier.'

They fell into a gloomy silence and drew long and hard on their water pipes. Again, he picked up the thread of the conversation and asked her about things that she preferred not to talk about.

'And what about him?'

She didn't answer. In fact, she didn't have any news of her husband. No one knew where he had disappeared to, or why. She was tired of people asking her about him. As far as she was concerned, he was just someone who had vanished from her life without a trace.

They avoided each other's eyes and her friend the Capricorn tried to change the subject. She liked wandering the city streets with him because he was easygoing and respected her long silences. As he walked by her side she was suddenly overcome by the feeling that still haunts her now: a feeling of emptiness and futility and a yearning to share her loneliness with another human being. Her Capricorn friend could talk endlessly. He told her all kinds of stories about the city's many squares and alleys and buildings. Sometimes he talked just to avoid the subjects that upset her. 'This is Bab al-Luq Square. Do you know why they call it that? People from across the city used to meet here. First it was called Bab al-Liqa – the Meeting Gate – then later Bab al-Luq.' She nodded her head for lack of anything to say. He narrated the history of the small, obscure cafés that they passed on their walk: 'This is the Sphinx Café. We used to come here after going to see a movie at Cinema Radio. Cinema Radio was something else in those days.' A few streets further on, he stopped and pointed. 'The Indian Cultural Centre is here, in this passageway. The Indian Teahouse is right next door. It used to be one of the loveliest cafés in the city. The intellectual crowd used to come here, but the artists mostly preferred the Rex Café on the corner of Imad al-Din Street.'

She had no idea where Imad al-Din Street was. The endless spider web of streets confused her, but she kept nodding her head encouragingly. 'Naguib al-Rihani and Stéphane Rosti and Anwar Wagdi used to go to the Rex. All the big film contracts were signed here – right here, on these very tables.' He swore to her that he once saw the actor Ahmad Mazhar sitting at the Rex. He was obviously very proud of the fact.

'My friend Yahya used to come here. His dream was to write a screenplay especially for Nadia Lutfi. Do you know what the café was originally?'

'What?'

'A barber shop,' he replied, grinning broadly.

He told the same stories every time but she didn't mind because, of all the people she knew, he alone still saw her as she imagined herself to be. To him, she never grew older and more abject with the passing days. He didn't notice the slight stoop she had acquired thanks to the painful stitches under her belly from the operation that followed her miscarriage. To him she didn't appear ashen and overweight and pitiful – quite the contrary. He said that she looked like Zubaida Tharwat, Soad Hosni, and Nancy Ajram all rolled into one. His presence was a source of delight to her. He made her feel beautiful in spite of everything.

She was in the habit of wearing a black, mannish blazer that she referred to a little sheepishly as 'sporty', but she really only wore it to hide things she would rather not think about, like her rear end, which kept getting bigger by the day. Her simple 'sporty' clothes screened off her fear of other telltale markers of her age, like her absent-mindedness, her impatience, her constant fatigue, her numerous delusions, and her insatiable need to walk and walk with no particular goal in mind. She tried to explain all this to him but couldn't make him understand.

She used to smoke her cigarettes slowly because she dreaded coming to the end of them. She would smoke them down to the filter, then stretch out on the bed, and the traces of chalk on her fingers and under her nails would fill her with a feeling of exhaustion. Sometimes, she prayed at night to ward off her loneliness.

She talked to him enthusiastically about the planets whenever she got bored of the story of the twin lions guarding Qasr al-Nil Bridge, or Princess Nazli's palace and Imad al-Din Street, or the Café of the Dumb. She said to him, 'I've cast your horoscope. Congratulations.'

'What does it say? Tell me.'

'It says that Jupiter is in the House of Capricorn this year. Jupiter is the planet of great fortune. It will be an exceptional year for you, my dear goat. Dust will turn to gold in your hands. All the planets are lined up behind you and every single month of the coming year will bring you good things. New horizons will open up before you, and many promises will be fulfilled. Now is the time to harvest fame and love and to exercise that masterful charm of yours to conquer the hearts of one and all.'

He laughed happily. He laughed so hard that his face became an indistinct blur.

'Do you really believe that stuff?'

'Sometimes I need to believe it.'

'And you? What does your horoscope say?'

'My friend the Cancer, you're at rock bottom!'

'You're always at rock bottom! Always hugging that bag of yours to your chest even when you're sitting down, as if you've got to hurry off for an appointment at any moment. You're always anxious. You never stay in one place for more than a few minutes. Do you know that Yahya never travelled in his whole life? The only time he set foot outside Cairo and went to Alexandria, he got into an accident and died.'

'Maybe. Who's Yahya?'

'Yahya, my friend. If he'd met you he would have really liked you.'

'Maybe.'

'And maybe then you would have stayed here forever and not thought about going away.'

'Maybe.'

They drew deeply on their water pipes when the silence fell between them and the smoky haze settled around their shared melancholy and wrapped it in a close veil. Then she picked up her bag, which was full of papers and chalk and desolation, and left.

Hend thinks about how she had never owned a suitcase in her whole life, how there were never any suitcases in their house, only huge wooden chests, left over from the days of the caravans that she had heard tell of and that her mother used for storing grain and other things. 'It's in the Nabulsi soap chest,' her mother would say with a hint of pride in her voice, or, 'It's on top of the trellis chest.' The chests grew old and tatty like everything else in their house. Rats scurried around merrily underneath them and the long years of neglect swathed them in an envelope of grease and enigmatic odours.

Her mother never owned a suitcase either. Hend wonders how she made the trip from her father's house to her husband's without any suitcases. It seemed that her mother had never travelled anywhere before her marriage. Even on those occasions when she got angry and put on her black dress, determined to leave the house forever, it never occurred to her to take anything with her. She would dry her eyes with a handkerchief as the children clung to the hem of her dress ('Mama, take me with you!'), but she never took anyone with her, for the simple reason that she never ended up leaving the house. She would go back into her room and shut the door fast behind her, and Hend's own girlish dreams of escape slowly collapsed under the weight of her mother's muffled sobs.

Her father owned a single small briefcase, but it wasn't made for travelling. It never occurred to him to leave the town bounded by small villages that he had grown up in. The case was full of papers: legal briefs and contracts and petitions that he had been entrusted with and that he took very seriously. He pored over them endlessly. It was a way of showing off how important he was, and also of proving to those who might want to forget it that he held a degree in law. But the truth was that he didn't give a damn about courts or briefs because he believed that everything could be solved by direct negotiation between the parties concerned. He didn't like to leave his house, and the times that Hend travelled with him were few and far between. The white Cadillac crossed the mud flats called Pharaoh's Springs; Shepherd's Hills, where communities of gypsies and nomadic Bedouins lived in canvas tents pitched on the edge of a brackish swamp; the Bedouin Estate, an endless sandy plain bordered by farms and small, isolated villages; the Lady's Estate; the Faridiya Estate; the Hill Estate; and the School Estate. The long green ribbon unwound itself along miscellaneous parcels of land until it emptied into the road that led to the gates of Cairo, that faraway city that people simply called 'Egypt'.

They entered the city from the east and the neighbourhood of Heliopolis, where most of her uncles lived (though Hend can no longer remember those long-ago visits that she paid them as a child). They always made the same stops: the pastry shop Gatineau, Omar Effendi, the fancy medical complex where they went for doctors' visits and lab results. They would while away the hour before one of these appointments at Groppi, the famous confectioner in Tal'at Harb Square. Her father would slowly sip his coffee as her mother finished up her window-shopping on nearby Qasr al-Nil Street. Her father loved to recount the origins of the names of the busy streets they walked down, especially the ones named after famous leaders of the nationalist movement, but in spite of his encyclopedic knowledge he somehow always managed to get lost. She recalled him stopping at the corner of Muhammad Mahmud Pasha Street, named after the leader of the Liberal Constitutional Party, and saying, 'He was a great man.' Her mother nodded her head knowingly as she tottered behind him in her high-heeled shoes. 'And this, my dear, is Sherif Pasha Street. Sherif Pasha oversaw the drafting of Egypt's first constitution and he was responsible for outlawing the slave trade.' Her mother sighed. She was thinking about things that were much more important than the history of Egyptian liberalism, things like doctors' appointments and lab results and shop display windows. She held Hend's wrist in a vice-like grip to keep her from running off and getting lost in the crowded, dangerous squares that were full of itinerant peddlers. The three of them stumbled around the maze of streets with a growing sense of claustrophobia. Her frustrated mother declared that the popular saying 'the person who built Cairo must have been a confectioner' was sheer nonsense and that God had thankfully spared them the hell of having to live in this city.

They took the road back home in a hurry. On the journey, her mother carried her on her lap. Her plump, soft legs were sheathed in velvety stockings and she wore a typical regional dress printed with big flowers and a blue coat lined with satin. The days were short and it got dark early, but they always went back the same night because her father was only comfortable sleeping in his own bed and because her mother had left half a dozen small kids behind and in any case driving at night was much more comfortable than driving by day. At night she missed the blue of the sky and her dreams of flight were thrown into sharper relief: 'Papa, I want to be an airline stewardess.'

'Over my dead body!' He laughed. 'No daughter of mine is going to wait on people.' She didn't understand what he meant by 'wait on people'. All she knew was that planes flew high up in the sky, and she could already picture herself as an elegant stewardess pulling a suitcase and a pile of dreams behind her. She fell silent for a while, then piped up again. 'Papa, I want to grow up and be an astrophysicist.' This time her mother answered wryly. 'You just want to fly off into space and leave us behind, don't you?' The cold wind came in through the window. She fell asleep on the way, and didn't see the small farms wrapped in the silence of the dark night.

The only time her father went on a long trip was to Mecca for the hajj. But he didn't stay long. He came back well before any of the other pilgrims – who inevitably fell in love with the noble lands of the Prophet – and he excused this shortcoming by declaring it to be 'an unlivable place. No wonder the Prophet emigrated!' Her mother interpreted this declaration as a manifestation of his eternal idleness. To her lasting chagrin, her husband had no desire to seek his fortune in the wealthy Gulf countries like everyone else. All he did was act strangely and endlessly hang around in reception houses, his own and other people's, always trying to solve problems that were no business of his. She was always complaining that he would never fix the universe, just fritter away his money – hers and the kids'. But she was afraid to tell him what was in her heart, and he refused to listen anyway. She would only sigh and dab at her tears and watch him from a distance as he sat every evening on the portico of the reception house on the hill and lit the fire and invited any and all who passed by on the path to come in for some tea. 'Please make yourself at home . . . you're welcome, by God . . .' Even after all his friends packed their suitcases and went off to find jobs in the oilfields, her mother still hoped that he could be persuaded to go too. Meanwhile, she overheard him declaring his firm intention to stay put to Doctor Shamil the pharmacist (who eventually decided to emigrate to Libya): 'Oh no, Shamil, I'm neither poor nor hungry – the hell with oil contracts! I've got a house of my own and my father's land from al-Sheikh to Ard al-Haysh. You go, and good luck to you, but me – never.'

And so the father stayed behind and tended the fire in front of the reception house, and Hend would sit next to him and say, 'Papa, I want to travel.' He told her that life was one big journey, and that she would certainly travel a lot, maybe even get altogether sick of travelling when she grew up. 'Papa will be a lonely old man by then and no one will want to keep him company any more.' He predicted that, by that time, he would no longer be able to see her when she stood before him because he would be blind, and would have to rely on his sense of smell to know his own daughter, his beloved daughter. Who knows, he would say, maybe her presence would even restore his sight, just like in the story of the Prophet Jacob, and then she would become a cane for him to lean on in his old age, and he would take her by the hand and they would walk together from way up on the hill down to the gypsy camps. These prophecies always made Hend laugh. Satisfied, her father would then move on to the story of the Prophet Joseph.

✶

Hend gazed at their house and it looked old and squat and decrepit to her because of the new, multi-storeyed buildings made from the red bricks fired in the kilns that had sprung up all over the surrounding marshland. Its old wooden roof could no longer support the stagnant rainwater that gathered in pools on cold winter days. Her mother hurried to put a tray with clay jars and a few brass pots under the holes in the living-room ceiling. She could hear the drops of water falling rhythmically into the receptacles at night, and the fire in the stove did nothing to warm the room packed with sleeping children. Her father came home late and she heard his slow steps approaching the door. He stopped in sometimes to check on the children wrapped in blankets that had grown worn and threadbare, and he sighed and rubbed his hands anxiously. In the morning he sat in the living room surrounded by his romping offspring and felt vindicated. 'Who would leave all these blessings behind for a bit of money?' he murmured to himself.

The 'blessings' gradually became bigger and their needs multiplied. The father made a few more signs advertising his expertise at the High Court of Appeals and distributed them in villages further afield. He took to calling the reception house his 'office' but he still wouldn't go abroad, even after all the other men in the village had gone. The people he knew dispersed – some of them to Iraq, others to the Gulf – and soon all kinds of imported velveteen blankets, soft and warm, could be seen hanging on the rooftop clotheslines, and stereo systems from Libya or TV sets from Dubai began to pop up everywhere. He would only smile at all these transformations – the suitcases that came and went to distant places – and shut himself up in his room with the following words on his lips: 'Whatever the Levantine wind brings, the Yemeni wind takes away.'

Maybe the mysterious phrase was meant for his wife, who had begun to cast an anxious eye on the tattered blankets and the clothes that she kept patching up time after time for the children, who were growing at breakneck speed. But she only nodded her head and held her tongue. Her father slipped his Maria Callas record back into the sleeve covered in writing that no one understood and settled down to smoke and read his book, *Liberalism and Egyptian Modernity*. He was careful that everything should remain just so: stable, distinguished, and tranquil, like the dreams that were growing before his eyes in the shape of his children. He never seemed to have any regrets, even after all the town's houses had emptied of their inhabitants, houses through which gigantic suitcases strapped in ropes came and went with the words scrawled on them in broad letters, such as: 'This bag belongs to Sayyid Abu Ibrahim who lives on the western bank in Mansha' or 'This suitcase is from the sons of Antar to their mother who lives on the White Estate'. And along with the traffic of travelling suitcases, the entire rhythm of life changed. Fatma al-Qarumiya no longer discreetly carried around her cloth bundle stuffed with odds and ends of women's clothing for sale. She began walking around town with a huge vinyl suitcase on her head that she would open on any random corner and call out, 'Sharjah satin! Imported nylon and silk! Blooming colours for lovely young girls! Abayas from the Hijaz, and the Prophet's musk!' And while the street across from their house was buzzing with the trade in imported goods, her mother continued to alter their old clothes to fit the next child down the line.

Hend wished she had a dainty red case of her own to take on

the long trip that she was sure to make one day. This was why she eagerly appropriated the white handbag that she found sitting in her mother's closet. Her mother let her have it because she never went out anyway, and no longer had any use for it. The bag was rectangular and had sharp edges, like those that hung on the arms of leading ladies in old movies. Hend put a comb and a mirror in it, as well as a few small bits of paper on which she'd written signed letters to herself, since everybody was writing letters to their absent relatives in those days. But hers were cold and lifeless and they mouldered away, unread, in the white handbag.

✡

Hend liked to talk about her father to the Capricorn. He had grown into her closest friend, and the spirals of fretful smoke that he blew out through his mouth made her think of her father. He reminded her of the old rush mats and the story of the Prophet Joseph, and his presence filled her with a feeling of warmth and security. He really listened to her when she talked, and she knew that he believed in her. She in turn found pleasure in his endless stories and the long walks they took together – just as she used to do with her father. She would fall into a kind of happy trance as she listened to him tell the same story over and over, in the same monotonous tone and with the same quiet enthusiasm. They met without reason or rhyme – they never actually made an appointment to meet – and she never had to weigh her words in his company, never felt self-conscious or obliged to hide her depression. He made her feel that he had been put on this earth just to make her happy, to dedicate his life to the sole purpose of walking with her along the meandering city streets. 'This is the Muhammad Ali Club, and this is the old Opera building. And this, my dear, is Jabalaya Street, where young lovers used to embrace in the dark. But they're all gone now. There are no more lovers in Egypt.'

He told her that he used to live on Mohandiseen Street with his friend Yahya. It was a quiet street, with hardly any traffic, only a few buildings owned by the Othman Company. He told her that Yahya used to like hanging around in Stella Bar, which was very different back then. Sometimes, when he walked a few steps behind her or hung on her every word, or expressed delight in her company, he reminded her of her son. He often said to her, 'If Yahya had met you, he would've fallen in love with you, and maybe then you would've been happier.'

She still didn't really know who Yahya was, but the repeated remark made her realise that he understood just how miserable and alone she was. She accepted it as an insight and a form of condolence, though sometimes it struck her as cruel, this yoking of her potential happiness to a dead man that she had never met. She attributed her bad luck to her zodiac.

It happens, she thinks to herself, that you're born on some summer night and suddenly find that you've been taken hostage by a star: always moving in the wrong direction, always pretending to be strong when in reality you quake in mortal fear, always wanting things but never reaching out for them, never knowing the difference between truth and illusion. It happens that a tentative, murky moon rises, a shape-shifting moon that slowly moves across the dome of the heavens, and your disposition grows dark and changeful like a chameleon. You cry and laugh at the same time, you love and hate at the same time. It happens that milk still seeps from her breasts because her brain has not sent the right signals to her glands. Milky clots cling to the inward-turned nipples, wells of hunger in which her star fate dwells, fast propagating and growing perhaps into small tumours like the ones that killed her mother. Would she die suddenly like her mother, she wonders.

The patterns traced by the stars give some measure of meaning to her life. She believes that the past and the future form a cosmic circle whose traces are inscribed on her forehead. She is possessed by the cruel certainty that providence and fate govern the world, and that men and women are powerless to change their destinies, as her mother had believed before her.

Hend can still picture her mother as she looked in her wedding photo, young and beautiful. Her uncles had carried her off one day, when night had fallen over that fertile green land, and the old Cadillac spirited her across peaceful deserts and wretched villages plunged into silence. It was summertime and the frogs croaked ferociously from their hiding places in the waterwheels. The car stopped on the long driveway along which electric lamps and coloured lanterns had been hung to welcome the new bride. Their steady hum scattered the thronging mosquitoes as the woman who would become her mother began to explore the old house that was now her home. The next morning she inspected the new clothes hanging in her closets. She put on the rose-coloured dress that revealed the fullness of her breasts and arms, and the rich ornaments that marked her noble ancestry — a necklace of real diamonds and a few gold bracelets in the form of snakes. A few years later she would sell them all to make ends meet.

The old house with the wooden roof was not as lovely as the new bride had imagined it to be, even after she hung her colourful curtains on the windows and a few paintings on the walls. Over the bed and the pillows that would soon grow wet with her tears she hung a painting of a naked and reclining houri of paradise. She hung a needlepoint canvas depicting a bowl of fruit overflowing with clusters of grapes behind the huge dining table, and another of a tearful child in the bedroom destined for the children to come. The perfume of a mango tree wafted in from behind the balcony as she dusted the cakes with sugar and set out the elegant cane chairs to make the new house worthy of her. Grandmother Zaynab sprinkled the marriage incense in every corner and the guests who had come to pay their respects gossiped about the young bride's hair, done up in small ringlets that delicately framed the edges of her face. Hend imagines that her mother must have been happy at first because she could turn on the radio and listen to all the songs that used to be forbidden to her: *Don't kiss me on the eye, eye-kisses divide lovers.*

Hend's grandfather's house was not far off but people frowned upon a young bride visiting her family, especially in the first years of marriage. They considered it to be a sign of the frivolity and rashness that ruin homes. In any case, Hend's mother could not remember her childhood fondly. Her father, who was also a Bedouin sheikh, married three women and sired many sons and daughters very close to each other in age. He insisted on sending his daughters to a convent school for a few years – as was the custom amongst the big families in the countryside in those days – so that they would learn to be obedient housewives. Her mother once showed Hend an old photo of some of her friends. 'This is the daughter of the mayor of Kafr al-Zayyat. And this is the daughter of the Bedouin chieftain al-Henadi Abd al-Hamid Bek Sultan. And this is the daughter of the mayor Lamlum Basil, my father's paternal cousin.' Her mother didn't remember much about her school days except for a few mysterious phrases in French that she had memorised: *Comment ça va? Très bien. Bon.* She used these phrases only in exceptional circumstances and when she wanted to show off her education – in conversations with doctors or strangers who came to visit, for example. She also liked to impress people with her exceptional talent for homemaking, which she gleaned from articles in ladies' magazines that she carefully copied into a notebook in which she kept her recipes for jam and preserves and vegetable casseroles and delicate flaky pastries. With the passing of time, and when the only talent required became the ability to feed seven mouths on a limited budget, these skills would become the object of general mockery.

After a number of years of useless schooling – as Hend's grandfather saw it – her mother and her sisters were given lessons at home by Madame Teresa, the seamstress who made their trousseaux: wedding dresses, honeymoon dresses, pregnancy dresses. Madame Teresa carried swatches of fabric around in her pockets and the girls would watch the rapid movement of her scissors in breathless silence as they cut out complicated double cloche and croisé patterns. The clothes were stowed away in boxes, along with the bars of soap and the perfumes and the velvety bedspreads and china and brass sets from Gattegno and

Cicurel and Sednaoui, and then they were carried off to the sound of jubilant ululations and the slaughtering of animals. Hend's grandfather did his best to treat all his daughters equally as they set off to meet their destinies, and yet he was fond of insisting that 'bringing girls into the world is a calamity that blackens the face and ruins the pocket'.

When it was Hend's mother's turn to make her grand exit from her father's house, she was more happily disposed than the other girls. The paternal cousin she had the good fortune to be marrying was clean-shaven and handsome, with a spotless white shirt. One of the servant girls had told her that he looked like Yusuf Bey Wahbi. He was a law student at Alexandria University, which meant that she would have to take extra care darning his socks and starching his shirt collars and ironing and scenting his handkerchiefs; she also spent a good deal of time embroidering his dressing gowns to befit his new status as a respectably married man.

The screams of the firstborn filled the house and the labour pains repeated themselves from one swollen belly to the next. The delighted grandfather, puffed up with pride, patted his grandsons on the back, slipped a few banknotes into his daughter's hand, ordered the animals to be slaughtered, then went back home. Five children later, Hend came into the world in the shape of a dark red crab, tormented by its ruling zodiac and its ascendant stars. Her father smiled and her mother murmured apologetically, 'Girls are sweet, though.' The grandfather didn't come this time, and no animals were slaughtered. By time Hend was born, her mother had grown much thinner and worn out from raising all those boys, from the constant din they made, from many a sleepless night. There were no more pregnancies after Hend, but her mother's face was always pale and exhausted, as though she had just completed a gruelling journey.

As soon as the mangoes ripened in the summer, Hend's mother would gather her six children into the old Cadillac and go forth on the 'journey of winter and summer', as her father sarcastically referred to it. His wife sat next to him and Hend sat in the back seat dreaming of faraway places that she had only ever heard of in stories, mysterious cities with brass domes wreathed in milky white clouds. Every year Hend eagerly waited for the moment when her mother would dab some perfume on her clothes, dust off the black cloak that she wore whenever she left the house, and pack up the jars of marmalade, the tins of home-made biscuits, and the freshly ground coffee that filled the kitchen with its delectable smell.

Hend would tug furiously at her mother's clothes: 'Take me with you!' Her grandfather's house wasn't far, just on the other side of a few empty enclosures and a couple of estates made up of cultivated and fallow land. The car rocked as the wheels pitched into the black mud. The gate of her grandfather's house creaked open slowly and the car passed through. The balcony, plunged in darkness and spread with colourful rugs, waited to receive them as they piled out of the car. Her mother smiled happily as she took in the sight of the kerosene lanterns hanging gaily in the orange orchards. She embraced her waiting sisters, who had also come from their husbands' houses, and they clung to each other in a protracted bout of mirth. Hend watched and listened. Her grandfather came out of his room and put out his hand to receive the shy, confused kisses of his progeny. The children held on to their mothers' dresses so that their grandfather could identify who they belonged to. He never caressed their hair or patted their heads; he only put out his hand to be kissed. On these trips, the world smelled of mangoes and vibrated with the buzzing of mosquitoes and the croaking of frogs glorying in the brackish waters of summer. The winter trip was shorter. The house echoed with the rustle of sluggish, lazy movement and the close rooms smelled of wood fires and Meccan incense. Even the games they played in winter were calibrated to the rhythms of the long, dark nights. The tales told were longer too, and more enchanting, and Hend would listen in wonder as she wandered feverishly through the corners of her unruly imagination. She dreamt of an old Cadillac, its windows open to the breeze, racing across unfamiliar lands and down endless streets, passing villages and dovecotes and mud houses, Bedouin tents and Pharaoh's Hills, and she fell asleep to the whistle of its wheels.

✫

She slept and woke to find that she had grown a few centimetres taller, and that her face in the mirror had acquired a new fullness. Her mother extricated her from the folds of her black cloak and pushed her away. Hend wept in despair at no longer being allowed to play with her male cousins or scramble up the mango trees bare-legged. They told her that her loud squeals of delight at being caught in a game of hide-and-seek were scandalous, and from then on she had to sit next to the Guest, picking at mounds

154

of cotton and twining wicks for the kerosene lamps, long slender wicks on which she hung her yearning to see the exotic places she heard about in stories.

The years passed and her mother grew more and more exhausted. Her aunts were busier than ever with their own affairs, and the journeys of winter and summer came to an abrupt halt: anyway, a woman's place was in her husband's house. Her mother sat in the western balcony and stared out into space while Hend wandered the dusty streets and alleys of the town and prowled around the gypsy camp nearby. Now, whenever she got angry she would say to her mother, 'I'm leaving. I'm leaving you all behind for good,' and run off to the gypsies. She cried herself to sleep on the straw-covered floor of their huts. She played Little House with the gypsy girls and laughed and romped in the straw. Then one day three pairs of arms snatched her up and took her away. Her brothers had worn themselves out looking for her all over town. When they finally brought her back home, her mother pounced on her and pinched her hard on the thigh. The pinch left a blood-red mark to remind her of the warning: 'No daughter of mine dares run away from her father's house.' So Hend only threatened to run away from then on. She would pack up her clothes in a cloth bundle like the ones the gypsy girls carried around and lay her tear-stained face down to sleep on it. 'I'm going,' she would whisper to herself, 'this isn't my home. No one here loves me.' Her mother laughed and called her a little sulker. 'All day long, acting like the gypsy girls and the servants,' she complained, 'and if anyone so much as opens their mouth, she packs her clothes and mopes around the house.'

On a pitch-black night in a small village in the furthest corner of the Delta, the frogs, revelling in the warm summer darkness, raised a ruckus in the pools of stagnant water and a little red gecko scurried along the wall of an old house. Mosquitoes came in through the open windows. Hend's mother, oppressed by the heat and her eternal solitude, leaned her aching back against the wall as the red gecko unfurled its tongue to snap up a mosquito. Hend grew to pity her mother's shattered dreams. She liked to talk to her friend the Capricorn about her mother, about the family's winter trip and summer trip, and she knew that he liked to listen to her. He watched her face tenderly and compassionately as she talked.

'I want to leave here now,' she said.

He responded with that steady, composed tone that drove her mad. 'You think leaving will make anything better?'

'Maybe I'll have better luck somewhere else.'

He shook his head as he drew on his water pipe, silently releasing the smoke through his nostrils in one long cloud. The expression on his face puzzled her. He broke the silence with the same old question: 'Have you written anything lately?'

She shook her head in the negative. 'I can't seem to.'

'Write about the winter trip and the summer trip.'

She laughed. She loved him because he believed in her, but her answer was always the same. 'Not now.'

'You remind me of Yahya.'

'Tell me about Yahya.'

'He was moody like you. I remember when he was in love with Nadia Lutfi.'

'What was he like?'

'I told you. Like you, moody.'

'I never liked Nadia Lutfi.'

'If he'd met you, he would have loved you more than Nadia Lutfi.'

'So what? How would that have changed anything?'

'Maybe you would've found what you've been looking for. And you wouldn't think of leaving.'

'I'm not leaving. I'm trying, just trying.'

'Maybe you would've fallen in love with him.'

'Maybe.'

'And maybe he would have chosen to stay too. To put off his death for a little while longer.'

She left him sitting there. She left Egypt too in a last-ditch attempt to escape everything that reminded her of her failure. She fled his attachment to her and the labyrinth of her own emotions. She crossed over to another continent without a word of farewell. She savoured her wretchedness and solitude. Pluto confronted her in stony silence, and Jupiter rested in the House of Capricorn: his house. She left without telling him that blessing and misfortune were defiantly conjoined in his stars; that their planets were fated to remain locked in opposing equilibrium, and that she knew he loved her.

Pluto moves into the House of Capricorn slowly. It will stay there for the next twenty-three years. It rumbles on its elliptical course through the galaxy, destroying worlds and rebuilding them. They call it 'the star of misfortune' because it is full of surprises, ponderous, lumbering, and wasted, like pain. It opposes her, threatening to rob her of all that she knows and loves and craves. She looks out through the window and watches the heavy rain splatter across the glass. Her heart beats faster and her dreams are full of terror of the unknown.

She watches her sleeping child with resignation. She embraces him and kisses his hand. A heavy weight presses down on her heart and the sudden contractions fill her with anxiety. She's afraid that he'll wake up alone and terrified, and search in vain for a body that should be lying next to him: 'Mama, where are you?' She's afraid of having to abandon him suddenly as her own mother abandoned her. That night she dreams that she is kissing her mother and the next morning desperately trying to shake her awake. 'Mama, where are you?' Her heart is still racing as she leaves a scrap of paper on the table next to him with a few phone numbers and a message – *Mom will be right back* – and descends the darkened stairs to go to the nearby hospital.

She sits in a long row of chairs waiting her turn. She moves between the oxygen masks and the blood-pressure meters and the heart monitors and stares at the long hallway full of doctors. She remembers a similar scene long ago – the same machines and the same medicine and food smells, the same white uniforms and glinting steel scalpels laid out on trolleys – and she is filled with dread. Her mother lay practically naked on a gurney, the thin wires of the heart monitor poking out of her chest. The little girl shrank away, terrified.

They wheeled Hend through the corridors of the hospital to the observation ward as she complained weakly that her chest hurt.

The doctor asks her, 'Do you have a family history of heart disease?'

'Yes,' she answers listlessly. 'My father died when he was forty.'

'Do you remember which month?'

'I think it was October or November. It was fall and school was about to start.'

'Tell me what happened.'

'He was telling me the story of the Prophet Solomon. Then suddenly he put his hand on his left shoulder and his heart stopped.'

'Was it at night?'

'Yes, around eight in the evening.'

'And your mother?'

'She died of breast cancer. Her breasts were always full of milk. My chest hurts too and the milk won't dry up. I've begun to forget things – a lot of things. Am I getting senile?'

'Is there something bothering you these days?'

'I'm always under a lot of stress, but this is the first time I've felt my heart racing like this. I feel it in my shoulder. I've begun to forget, and I don't want to forget. Do you know Hemingway?'

'Yes.'

'Hemingway began to lose his memory too. He couldn't write any more because he was losing his memory. I want to write. Am I going to become like him?'

The doctor laughs. She asks Hend to put on her clothes. 'I think you're worrying too much. In any case I'll look at the test results. We'll be in touch if there's anything to be concerned about.'

She takes the sedatives and leaves. She walks alone down the dark street. Her heartbeat still hasn't calmed down. She opens the door of the house and finds him still asleep in bed. She tears up the piece of paper that she left for him.

She tries to sleep. She dreams that her mother is caressing her hair. In the dream, she weeps bitterly. Her mother wakes her and says, 'Go to your son.' She asks herself why God torments mothers with milk that won't stop flowing.

The child gets out of bed and puts his arms around her. 'Mom, did you go out last night?' He asks her this as though she's sitting in the witness box, in a commanding tone or perhaps an anxious one, as though his whole existence depends on her being there by his side. She answers him firmly.

'I was here.'

He rubs the sleep and worry from his eyes, then says, 'I dreamt that you went out while I was asleep.'

'But I was here, darling,' she repeats soothingly.

'I dreamt that I woke up and didn't find you.'

'I'm right here, my love.'

She bursts into stinging tears. She rages against Pluto and death, the robber, and childbirth and her own self. She cries bitter tears, and her heart shudders as though it's about to grind to a halt.

Her son puts his arms around her heaving waist. 'Mama, what's the matter?'

'I can't breathe.'

He pulls her by the hand and makes her lie down on the bed and relax. She takes one of the sedatives but it only makes her cry more, and she says to him, 'I had one friend in the whole world. He was kind and gentle. He was born one day under the sign of Capricorn. He died today.'

'Your friend?'

She nods her head. It's the way of the world, always losing something, always living in the hope of discovering a truth that doesn't exist.

Her son hugs her close, as though their roles were reversed, she the child and he the parent. 'Don't be sad, my darling Mama. I'm here with you.'

She hugs him tight and cries on his shoulder. Suddenly her only son becomes her one true friend.

Prospect Park

Flatbush Avenue converges with a half-dozen other streets at a spot called Prospect Park, or 'The Tranquil Garden'. They say that Prospect Park was designed to be a smaller version of Central Park – the giant green space that sits in the centre of Manhattan – and that all its saplings came from there. They say that the park was first planted soon after the Brooklyn Bridge was finished. It used to be a hamlet surrounded by Dutch poultry farms, vineyards, and dairy factories, then, after the bridge was built, it became a suburb of Brooklyn. Over the years its picturesque Dutch architecture attracted writers and composers and bohemians of all kinds. Real-estate agents intent on demonstrating the appeal of Brooklyn are sure to point out to you the house that Arthur Miller lived in: 'His young wife Marilyn Monroe lived with him in this very building before she became a star. And this is Henry Miller's house. He's the author of *Tropic of Capricorn*. Paul Auster still lives and works here in Brooklyn, and this is the tree that Betty Smith wrote her famous novel about.' And in other places they stick up posters of the John Travolta film *Saturday Night Fever*. And the real-estate agents will remind you of all of them if you're looking for a room suitable to house your dreams.

Hend has learned the map of Park Slope by heart. It helped that a lot of people she met liked to talk about the history of the neighbourhood. Many of them were dreamers constantly on the lookout for that one person who would discover their talent, always poring over their notebooks in some early morning café and waiting for inspiration to seize them. They always looked as though they were on the point of recreating the universe. At night, they eagerly sought out the stray journalist or editor in urbane establishments like Coco Bar and Exotic Bar and the Tea Lounge. Hend rarely set foot in those places. They were way too expensive and she dreaded the kind of attention that a woman by herself might attract. She hurried past them on her daily route – a route that took her nowhere.

Atlantic Avenue is home to a host of Arab-owned stores. Narak the Armenian's shop is on a street to the south of the avenue, close to the park. Narak sells chessboards and novelty chess pieces, as well as books about the game. He also gives lessons to anyone who wants them. Passers-by stop at his place, especially kids on their way to the park, drawn by the whimsical shapes of the chess pieces, some of which have storybook themes, like Snow White and the Seven Dwarfs. The smiling Armenian relishes the delight of the children around him. They remind him of his days at the Scientific Renaissance Secondary School in Baalbek, where he used to teach art before emigrating to America. His patience was legendary. He would sit for hours teaching the kids the basic principles of the game by way of a set of magical mathematical formulas.

When Hend goes for a walk in the evening her son stays a few steps ahead of her, grave-faced and contemplative, in an effort to prove to his mother that he's grown up now and capable of going out by himself. He gets all kinds of crazy ideas, like changing his first name because it isn't 'cool' enough. He doesn't like his last name either. He wants to call himself Ben, colour his hair blond, and spike it with gel to make it look like Iron Man's. The pimples that have begun to pop up on his forehead upset him terribly. He calls them 'acne' in English and spends inordinate amounts of time fixing his hair so that it hides his forehead. He examines his skin in the mirror and decides he likes it because it's 'tan' and his friends envy him. One day he says to her, 'How come you don't look for *a decent job*?' The word *decent* confuses her. It takes her a minute to figure out what it means in Arabic – 'respectable' – and she bristles with resentment. 'Why don't you think about your own future and leave me alone,' she replies sharply. Truth be told, she wishes she could find that kind of job. She'd like to be a painter or a writer or even an actress. She still dares to hope that some dreams at least can come true at any age.

When they get to the chess shop she leaves him sitting by himself at the table that Narak points to, and goes to sit across the street, on one of the broad, hospitable, rose-tinted stone stoops that descend down to the pavement from the elegant old brownstones. She watches Naguib al-Khalili as he sits at a table in front of the shop in his grey suit, clutching one of his manuscripts and scribbling furiously. She smiles at him and he smiles back, but she doesn't approach him because she knows that he's always desperate for someone to talk to in Arabic – and then there's no stopping him, the same old monologue that leaves her exhausted: how he came to America from a village near Nablus and opened his store, The Groom's Sweets, in 1955; how he covered the walls

164

in pictures of his old village and how the store became famous for its old-school rose-water sherbet and Nabulsi kunafa stuffed with cheese and its small round honey cakes. Every morning the local Arab workers flocked to The Groom's Sweets to buy the cakes that tasted of home and an obscure longing that they struggled to understand.

After decades of gruelling work, Naguib al-Khalili now spent most of his time at his friend Narak's shop. He decided to retire when his nephew arrived in his turn in Brooklyn and gradually took over the bakery. His nephew is a tall, thin young man called Ziyad. He always dresses in black from head to toe and wears a Palestinian kufiya around his neck. Ziyad came to America to study film-making, but the real world got the better of him and he began to work full-time in the bakery with his uncle, ordering the sheets of dried apricot and making the fig pastries stuffed with pistachio exactly according to their original recipes because the customers would have nothing else. The customers come back again and again for a fleeting taste of their childhood. The Nabulsi kunafa is stuffed with real halloumi cheese and the amount of honey in the baklava is always just right. The lady fingers are delicate and crunchy, the red-rose sherbet smells of mountain flowers, and the bitter orange jam might have been aged in your own grandfather's basement, God rest his soul, whatever his name was. Everything reminds them of the smells and tastes of sweet and distant places and times.

Memory thrives on details – details that al-Khalili safeguarded and preserved, and now Ziyad too: flexible, cunning details like the crispiness of a single square of sweet kunafa. Ziyad washes his hands of the day's fatigue and tries not to think about his increasingly unlikely dreams. He watches movies with his uncle in the evening – classics or blockbusters – or they go to the theatre or an art gallery. Al-Khalili will laugh and say to Ziyad, 'The boy's turned out just like his uncle – an artist by God, my son! What else but the love of art brought us here from our country? Your uncle Narak adored painting and playing the violin, and I used to think I was the prophet Gibran or Mikhail Nu'ayma and that I would write all the poems that Ibn Zaydan himself, God rest his soul, never managed to write. But exile is a son of a bitch, Ziyad, and in the end it only gives you what you've got coming to you anyway.'

Ziyad hangs his head. He tries to understand but all he can think about is the film that he dreams of making: a film about Brooklyn's Arab-American community and the domestic problems they face. Like his uncle, Ziyad adores T. S. Eliot's *The Waste Land* and Walt Whitman's *Leaves of Grass*. He knows Lorca's poems about Harlem and the Brooklyn Bridge by heart. He is always busy gathering material for his film and planning the scenes that are supposed to take place on the bridge's pedestrian walkway; always thinking about things like funding and shooting and auditioning actors and actresses. He jots down ideas and observations in a small notebook that he keeps in his pocket as he sits behind the counter in The Groom's Sweets. The bakery is a good place to study the different types of Arab immigrants. He considers it to be the source of his inspiration. Naguib al-Khalili loves to boast about this cultured nephew who has filled his life with novelty. Ziyad and his Armenian friend are all he has left in the world.

Both Narak and Naguib used to teach at the Scientific Renaissance Secondary School. Later, they travelled across the world together. They still take pleasure in sitting and reminiscing about those long-ago days. They remember the crowds of Palestinian refugees spread out on the grass in the meadows of Baalbek and endlessly discussing how they would return to their villages once the war was over. When one of the men said he didn't think they would be able to go back till at least a year or two after the end of the war (this was in 1948), the others jumped in with long encomiums on the Arab armies that would surely win the war in a matter of days. They were so certain that the war would end quickly that some of them had even fed their chickens and cows as usual just before fleeing their homes. Many years passed while the men fought over their predictions. Naguib al-Khalili grew up and Narak turned into a handsome young man who loved to paint and play the violin. He dreamt of going to Egypt and watching the great Naguib al-Rihani in *The Education of Girls* at Cinema Rivoli on Imad al-Din Street. The two friends went to Egypt together, then decided to travel even further. Narak started looking for passage on a ship to New Jersey, where his cousins lived. Naguib was also becoming more and more convinced that the return to his village in the Galilee might take longer than he had hoped and that it would be better to work while he waited. So they boarded a boat together in Cyprus and set sail for the land dreamt of by intrepid explorers.

Narak joined his cousins in the grocery business and Naguib took a job as a baker in the shop that now bears the name The Groom's Sweets. Al-Khalili saved every penny he earned so that he could go back and get married in his village once he had rebuilt his father's house, which would no doubt need a lot of repairs after the war. The war lasted for a long time and Naguib forgot all about marriage and the return. His main concern now was to put aside enough money to cover his father's living expenses back in Baalbek and his sister's too. She had stayed on in the village of Sahmata, adamant that she would never leave her country. Naguib fretted about money and worked like a dog, work that never seemed to end, except when life had finally passed him by and the dreams he had slaved to realise had evaporated into thin air. People who knew him said that he lived an ascetic life, never changing his dull grey trousers and his red checked shirt except on very rare occasions. He didn't smoke and didn't eat much, nor was he in the habit of indulging in games like dominoes or dice in the Arab cafés. He didn't like hanging around in coiffeuses and usually went to bed early, though once in a while he liked to smoke a water pipe because he believed that it strengthened the memory and cleaned out the intestines. Naguib's voice was always pitched low and he steered clear of the dictionary of curses that revolved around mothers and sisters by lowering his head and keeping to himself. He was never known to laugh out loud and, according to many of his oldest friends, he was still a virgin, having never known a woman, having never known anything but the longing to return.

In the old photos from Baalbek during the war, Narak and Naguib sit side by side in the meadow, Narak holding his violin and Naguib looking young and handsome with his pitch-black eyes and gentle, regular features. His hair is slicked back in a Clark

Gable cut and he wears a spotless white shirt open at the collar, a stylish blue jacket tailored at a shop in the La'aziya Building in Beirut slung over his shoulder. The memories faded away one by one as the years passed, and so did the dream of return, the only thing remaining of his identity proclaimed in a sheaf of old papers stamped 'Palestinian refugee, place of residence: Baalbek, Lebanon'. Now there was no question of going back. Now he complains of life in general, and that America is nothing but a big lie. He has developed endless theories about how New York is like a giant meat grinder, its rusted gears immediately tossed in the garbage. He believes that people are not as free here as Americans like to claim — money and survival form the axis on which everything turns. 'What kind of life is it that forces you to bow down to a customer just because he hands you a few pennies? Maybe you dream of buying a house or raising children, but you're sure to end your days paying off the mortgage and the college loans, and you might even die before you manage it.' His words usually collide with the opinions of Mr Muhammad, the waiter in the Arabian Nights coffee shop, who doesn't like this kind of talk, and says so: 'If you're not happy here, why don't you leave, brother? No one is forcing you to live in the land of the invaders, Abu Zayd!'

The new arrivals mostly agree with Mr Muhammad. They needle Naguib wickedly because his endless homilies and the self-pity in his eyes bore them. The younger ones make no allowances for his age and experience and the decades of hard work that have worn him out. He usually answers their comments in a gentle, sad voice. 'Boys, if any of you knows of a place for me back home, I wish he'd send me off on the first ship.' So they let him be and the young men avoid sitting with him so as not to have to listen to his talk about the city's heartlessness and inhumanity, the number of vagrants and homeless people that wander its streets, the old people in the parks neglected by children who have no time for anything but making money. He can often be heard wondering aloud about the kind of city that could produce all this human misery, this city that people call the apple of the world; a fortress of tyranny and slavery, just like all those other cities of old that had crumbled into dust.

There is no longer any place for him in the coffee shops of Bay Ridge because no one likes having him around; his talk depresses and irritates them. So he has chosen this corner of Park Slope, far from Bay Ridge and its Arab neighbourhoods. He sits at Narak's chess table and eagerly follows the movements of the marvellous stone pieces, Snow White and Hercules and the Japanese Chu Shogi wedges. His childlike delight in these games draws him like a magnet to the shop day after day. But most of all he enjoys the company of his quiet Armenian friend, who is often busy fiddling with his musical instruments – the oud or the violin. Layla Murad's voice wafts through the genial Armenian's shop and feelings of peace and contentment flutter in the folds of their shared silence. Together, they recall the hoopoes of Nablus or that species of fig bird that they used to call the parson because of its crown of black feathers.

Naguib al-Khalili graduated with a degree in Arabic. In those days, Arabic teachers were given an extra stipend and the money allowed him to complete his studies at the High Institute of Teachers in the neighbourhood of Dokki in Egypt. He and his friend Narak went to Egypt in the early 1950s and they shared an apartment on Nawal Street in Dokki for two years. On the return journey from Port Said to Beirut via Cyprus they saw the ships, and from that day on they dreamt of crossing the oceans and seas. Finally, one day they did just that and never came back.

Al-Khalili has always been enamoured of poetry and literature and film and so he never wonders at his nephew Ziyad's passion for making movies. He says to him in the Egyptian accent that he never entirely lost, 'You're a natural, just like your uncle.' Ziyad — who catches glimpses of the family's artistic future lurking behind the sacks of flour and sugar in the stockroom of The Groom's Sweets — smiles, and his uncle pats his hand affectionately. These days al-Khalili is busy with what he likes to call his life's work: a linguistic study of the most common errors in Arabic composition. He adores grammar, almost as much as he adores Layla Murad's voice and Charlie Chaplin movies.

He was famous for his ability to solve any problem related to parsing and declension, and when he was a young man everyone said that he was sure to make a good teacher one day. Naguib al-Khalili was a great admirer of the prominent Egyptian philologist Hasan Zaza. Zaza had studied classical philology in France and was proficient in more than twenty languages. He was a Jew, and the story goes that when his professor at the Sorbonne insisted that a Jew could not live safely in Egypt, Hasan Zaza — who was about to defend his dissertation proposal at the time — replied, 'Come with me to Egypt and you'll see for yourself. You can walk around the streets wearing your yarmulke and people will greet you as "Khawaga Sednaoui" or "Khawaga Luca" and treat you with the utmost respect.' Naguib al-Khalili dreamt of following in the footsteps of this Egyptian professor whose life story he knew by heart. He had a lot of other dreams too but he had ended up as a baker with a talent for making Nabulsi pastries. He considered this job to be the art of shaping the nostalgia that tugged at the heart strings of the Lebanese and Syrians and Palestinians who lived at the edges of Brooklyn.

Al-Khalili has held on to a small part of his faded dreams in the form of an old black school bag that he still carries with him everywhere. No one has a clue why he has carried it around all these years, or exactly what it contains, and the strange black bag only adds to his reputation as an old eccentric. Even his old friend Narak often wonders why he holds on to all those ancient books, books with titles like *Shards of Gold in the Explanation of the Language of the Arabs* and Sibawayh's *Grammar* and Ibn Malik's *Alfiya*. There is even an original manuscript written out in his own hand called *A Summary of Foreign and Loan Words in the Arabic Language*, with his name, Naguib al-Khalili, inscribed in a ponderous Kufic script under the title. Every morning he comes to sit at the table in front of Narak's chess shop and takes out his books. He will go over some complicated grammatical rules so as not to forget them, or repeat a few lines of poetry to sound out their metre, and he can often be heard cursing the exile that has made him forget the rules that govern the negative and the possessive construct. Narak sits inside watching his friend as he works away at his manuscript on grammatical mistakes. Al-Khalili's usually soft voice rises a couple of notches as he calls out to ask his friend about an obscure point of classical declension. Narak, who used to be an art teacher not a language teacher, isn't much interested in the rules of grammar. His dreams lie elsewhere. But, as everyone knows, the ship that sets sail for the east may well be driven by the wind in the opposite direction. Narak's business is on the point of collapse: customers are few and far between, as whimsical chess pieces aren't so much in demand any more. These days nobody cares about those exquisite, miniature works of art lovingly hand-sculpted by craftsmen like himself. Narak is convinced that New York has become a city inhabited by people just passing through, people who don't give a damn about art, or one-of-a-kind chess pieces. Even the number of tourists has dwindled, the winters are getting colder every year, and the warehouses are overflowing with unsold stock. Narak grieves at his son's refusal to take over the shop. The boy has begun to suggest all kinds of schemes for starting another business there. Sons wait patiently for their parents to die so they can follow their own dreams, and that's the way of the world. The thought makes Narak, who knows and loves every single piece in his shop, terribly sad. The way of the world is never fair.

✳

Hend sits on a stoop across the street from the shop. Ziyad passes by, just as he does every evening, and says hello. Hend likes the sound of his deep, mellow voice. She likes his youthful, clean-shaven features, his nicely groomed hair, his dark, stylish clothes, and the smell of his skin. Hend likes Ziyad, but when he passes by she pretends to be busy writing something or other. Sometimes he sits down next to her and she wishes she could confess to him that she really isn't writing anything at all, that she's just pretending. She wishes she could tell him that her notebook is full of poems that she's collected, poems she wishes she had written herself. Instead she lowers her eyes and reads to him ('Come, my darling, I am the lush hyacinth soon to be plucked by autumn . . . take me between your hands and hold me close, covering my face with kisses'). He asks who the author is and she tells him that it's a verse from a poem by a Pashtun poetess, a woman just like her. Ziyad is oblivious of her hint. His mind is forever on the film he's going to make. He tells her about how Quentin Tarantino, one of his favourite directors, used to work in a store just like him. True, the store was a video store – but in the end it was a store. Tarantino obviously used the opportunity to study people and watch movies and talk to his friends about cinema. Then he became a star. 'That's America for you,' says Ziyad, 'a land of miracles.' Suddenly he asks her, 'Have you seen *Pulp Fiction*?' She has no idea what he's talking about, so he repeats the question in Arabic and he even translates the title. She hasn't seen it, she tells him. She wants Ziyad to understand that they are interested in the same things, that she loves movies too (though she prefers Egyptian ones from the fifties), and that she especially likes the kind of movies that are about married couples and jilted wives. Ziyad leaves quickly before she can read the rest of her poems to him, poems she's collected for him.

Hend gazes blankly towards the park frequented by old people, unserviceable people who now spend their days sipping therapeutic drinks and nibbling on sandwiches alone on empty benches. They look for a spot in the sunshine and gingerly sit down, trying hard to ignore the aches and pains of rheumatism, of loneliness and old age. They contemplate that small paradise surrounded by gigantic trees coming to life again after a long, cold winter – a cruel place in spite of its beauty for those coming to the end of their long journey. If the weather is fine, they sit and gaze at the many-coloured cherry and mulberry trees, the chestnuts and oaks, while people jog around the park and young mothers with strollers congregate to spend the morning playing with their children. Hend watches her son in the chess shop from across the street.

Lilith arrives at the Armenian's shop and Naguib al-Khalili grows flustered and confused like a schoolboy with a crush as he hurriedly wipes down the chair next to him with his handkerchief. Lilith smiles and the tiny wrinkles criss-crossing her small face spring to life. She gropes for words that constantly elude her now that her memory has been snatched away by old age. Al-Khalili describes her with unparalleled zeal: 'She's a real lady. There isn't another woman in this whole country as sweet or as perfect.' Every day Lilith comes to the shop and sits down opposite him wearing a spotless coat and expensive perfume and jewellery that she changes from one day to the next. She gives off an air of stately elegance and she never gets bored or interrupts his long meandering reminiscences. Her brief comments are always simple, her speech always deliberate and refined. The serious and wistful expression on her face is there thanks to the giant eraser that has wiped away most of her memory. These days she has to make a supreme effort to hold on to essential bits of information like her name, her address, and the name of her only son. She carries all her important papers with her in the pocket of her coat but she's terrified most of the time that she'll lose them or forget them, and every few minutes she feels her pocket nervously to make sure they're still there. She also keeps a small notebook in which she jots down the things she wants to remember, things such as her son and grandchildren's names and the numbers of her bank accounts. She writes other things in a clear hand on little snippets of paper and then forgets where she's put them. ('Erika is my son Omar's wife.' 'My name is Layla al-Sa'id and they call me Lilith.') But in spite of all her precautions, her memory still fails her, and she wastes hours rummaging in her handbag and her pockets for these stray bits of paper. She is proudly and stubbornly engaged in a running battle with senility. This is why she spends a lot of time making sure every hair on her head is in place and that her coat is always spotlessly clean, and also why she prefers to remain perfectly quiet rather than open her mouth and trip up on her words.

Naguib al-Khalili, who often wonders why he feels so light and happy in Lilith's presence, watches her approaching from a distance and stands up respectfully as she draws closer. He loves talking to her. He talks and talks and she listens. He talks about the time he spent in Egypt when he was a student at the High Institute of Teachers, and about Professor Hasan Zaza and the boat from Port Said to Cyprus. He says to her, 'I stayed at the Andalusia Hotel, do you know where it is? It was one of the nicest hotels in Cairo in those days. Hot water and ice-cold water and Sudanese waiters who wore the cleanest clothes I've ever seen — cleaner even than the uniforms worn by the king's servants, madam!' Lilith smiles a little and stares dreamily into the distance. 'I went to the spice market – have you been to the spice market before?' He answers his own question. 'No, I guess not, you look like a real lady, so why would you frequent those old, dilapidated markets? You see, when I went to Cairo I didn't know anyone. I went with Narak.' He points to his friend, bent over the strings of a violin inside the chess shop. 'He was an artist back then too and as soon as he got to Cairo he started asking everyone where the great composer Muhammad Abd al-Wahhab lived, while I ran around looking for a place for us to rent. Of course, "the stranger's eye is feeble", as they say. As soon as I left the hotel I ran into a well-dressed young man who asked me if I wanted to buy an expensive Rado watch. He said that he needed the money badly and that he was willing to part with it for five pounds, even though it was worth five hundred. In those days five pounds was the equivalent of more than forty Lebanese lira – enough money to live on for a whole month! But, like I said, the stranger's eye is feeble, even if he's smart as a whip. And so, madam, I bought it. Then Narak came back and said, "Naguib, they've cheated you, this watch is worthless." Being an Armenian, Narak understood absolutely everything, but I scolded him anyway: "You left me all this time to look for Mr Muhammad Abd al-Wahhab's house," I said, "and we can't afford to stay at the Andalusia for much longer. We have to find an apartment." And so Narak and I starting looking together for an apartment close to the centre of town. We went to an agent on Nawal Street in Dokki and afterwards we drank a fantastic cup of coffee at the Indiana Café. I'll never forget it my whole life.'

Lilith nods her head and doesn't say a word. If she says anything, it will be something from left field like, 'Oh, of course I remember Nawal . . . of course.' From time to time she dabs at her face with a scented handkerchief. She checks her short, carefully cut grey hair in a little mirror or feels around in her pockets every so often to make sure that she still has the papers with her address and her son's phone number in case she gets lost. But she never loses her way. She just sits in front of Narak's shop and doesn't think of going anywhere else. She listens closely to this man who talks about faraway people and places, and smiles. Her dark pupils shine with pleasure and tears of nostalgia swim in Naguib al-Khalili's old eyes. He wipes them away with the handkerchief that he keeps in his pocket, and goes on with his stories.

'And then, madam, when the waiter at the Indiana Café (where only distinguished people used to go) told us that Muhammad Abd al-Wahhab sometimes came there to meet his friends, Narak and I started going there too every day. The waiter said that he came to the café incognito, all bundled up in a black coat and hat, but that we would know him right away. "He's tall and thin and never greets anyone and doesn't drink coffee either, only anise." He told us that he was very paranoid and always pestered the waiters to make sure his glass was clean.'

Layla Murad's voice comes drifting out of the shop where Narak sits listening to his friend telling the story of their lives to the strange lady called Lilith. He still likes hearing the story from Naguib's lips. Al-Khalili goes on.

'We used to spend two whole pounds on a single cup of coffee. Like I said, the Indiana Café was one of the fanciest cafés in Cairo and we were just students back then, but only bees know how to make honey, my good lady, or so I said to Narak, who's sitting in the shop behind you right now. In those days he looked like Anwar Wagdi, all elegance and shining black hair – and he still does!' Naguib laughs as he looks at his old friend, then he says, 'But he can't hold a candle to you, madam – "though the flower may fade, its perfume lingers on".' Lilith smiles again and he can't tell whether she's smiling because she's understood the compliment or simply to share in his own laughter. Her decayed memory has made her shy and quiet and inscrutable. Naguib wonders whether she's even capable of putting a meaningful sentence together. Whenever she tried to share in his reminiscences about how beautiful Cairo was, for example, she only managed to repeat a random phrase whose ring happened to please her. 'Beautiful . . . it was beautiful,' she would murmur, then lapse into a sad silence, or a happy one; she never attempted to add anything else, and her eyes gleamed mournfully. Naguib al-Khalili pauses and smiles gently into the sudden silence, then picks up the thread once again.

'Next, my good lady, I met a nice man who treated me just like his own son. We started meeting at the Rex Café downtown and going for long walks together through the city he knew so well. One day he invited me to lunch at a local grill house in the old Hussein district. I don't remember the name of the place any more, but by God, madam, I can still taste the delicious food I ate there on the tip of my tongue. Meanwhile, Narak kept hanging around the Indiana and paying two pounds every day for a cup of coffee in the hope of meeting the great composer. One day a man who fit the waiter's description – tall, silver-haired, and wearing a black coat – came in and ordered coffee. The waiter came over to tell Narak that the person he was looking for had finally arrived. Lo and behold, Narak gets up, runs over to the tall man in the black coat, covers his hand in kisses, and says, "I've been waiting for you for a long time, maestro!" The tall man answers him with exaggerated politeness, "I'm Abdel Warith Assar, son!"' Naguib laughs as he glances at Narak in the back of the shop, and they exchange wry smiles. 'Of course you know who Abdel Warith Assar was,' he says to her. 'A very great actor.'

Lilith smiles that obscure smile of hers again. Perhaps she likes the story, or perhaps she's just homesick. All that al-Khalili knows about Lilith is that she's Egyptian – he knows this from the few words that she's let drop. He also knows that she has a son somewhere or other; he doesn't know what his name is, but his young American wife, Erica, sometimes comes for her at the end of the day. She wears a heavy hijab and pulls one child by the hand as she pushes a small stroller with sleeping twins in it with the other. Erica is always in a hurry. She rushes about looking for her crazy mother-in-law and declares that she's losing her mind from always having to follow her around. But Erica doesn't lose her mind because she always finds Lilith looking cool and calm as a cucumber; only her hands tremble a bit. She waits quietly for her to get up and follow her, and she never looks at Naguib al-Khalili, who watches the back of her long Islamic cloak recede into the distance as she walks away with Lilith in tow.

Lilith's apartment looks out onto the park. Her house reflects her love of elegance and her obsession with detail: an antique Persian carpet, gaberdine bedspreads, embroidered sheets and Arabian pillows, antique furniture and records of all kinds. Lilith lived by herself for many years, but ever since she began to lose her memory, her son and his wife and their three children are always hovering around. Her son is Omar Azzam, the young man that the Arabs on Fulton Street all talked about. His exemplary piety and the great wealth that God saw fit to give him were legendary. They praised him as an example of filial rectitude, especially Abd al-Karim, who liked to say, 'A righteous son is the best provision against the ups and downs of this world . . . especially in this damned exile where everything fades – health and beauty and style – and the only thing you're left with is a lost and wandering mind, like Lilith's. A good boy is a blessing in those circumstances.' He swears by God almighty that if it hadn't been for her son, she would have been reduced to roaming around with the homeless people in the neighbourhood and sleeping in the park.

When people asked Lilith how she came to this country, she would tell them a lot of different stories. She was from an aristocratic family – her grandfather was the Minister of Irrigation in the cabinet of Adli Yakan, the leader of the Liberal Constitutionalists. She had never been what people call a beautiful woman. She was petite and thin and dark-complexioned. She religiously followed all the latest fashions and bought all the latest records, especially Frank Sinatra and Liza Minnelli. She loved to dance too. She married early and got pregnant right away. Her husband was a famous doctor with a big private clinic in Bab al-Luq. His practice was frequented by movie stars and all of Cairo's elite families. He had been trained in France and was related to Abdul Rahman Hassan Azzam – one of the most important Arab intellectuals of the twentieth century according to many.

Lilith had everything she could possibly want, but happiness is a mysterious and wayward thing. People talk a lot about the particular madness of women, but they had never seen a woman as mad as Lilith before. Lilith lived in a small mansion on the banks of the Nile in the suburb of Garden City. Her life was as ordered and picturesque as an oil painting. Her husband spoiled her no end (he called her his 'little kitten') and his family often reproached him for giving her too much freedom. 'Lilith is an artist and an important society lady,' he would chuckle on these occasions. 'She isn't a little girl any more.' She would sit in the sun at the Hunting Club wearing her Jackie Kennedy sunglasses, or ride horses and go for long swims in the pool in one of her many designer bathing suits, or go to cocktail parties and mingle with famous actresses at catwalk shows. Then she gave birth to her only son, Omar, whom she named after Omar Sharif in the hope that he too would one day become a famous actor. She had adored his last film with Barbra Streisand, *Funny Girl*, and like all the girls of her class, she was crazy about anything to do with Hollywood and Broadway.

The birth of her son changed her dramatically, even though she had plenty of help raising him: his paternal grandmother devoted all her time to the boy and there was an army of nannies in the house. Lilith refused to nurse the child in order not to ruin her breasts and she rarely took him in her arms. She grew headstrong and sullen. She smoked a lot and slept all the time, refusing to see her son or her husband or anyone else for that matter. She would rage and cry for no apparent reason. Her husband turned the rooms on the roof of the house into a pretty studio for her to paint in and he pruned the jasmine bush so that its branches would cover the walls with fragrant blossoms. He kept her company every evening and he sent for the latest records to quench her thirst for music. Their life together would have seemed ideal if not for people's gossip about the husband's many affairs. Lilith never once discussed this subject with him. She was, after all, a refined society lady who looked down on such trivial matters, but she gradually lost her vivacity, her joy in the world, and a sense of her place in it. One spring evening, when a gentle breeze shook the jasmine blossoms loose and made them fall to the ground and give off their delicate scent, Lilith stood at the window of her room and realised that she could no longer pretend to be happy. A record turned on the gramophone and Frank Sinatra sang about learnin' the blues.

She had no idea why she suddenly burst into tears or where this feeling of longing that shook her had come from. There was no other man in her life; she never even thought about love any more. Perhaps it was the ache in Sinatra's voice that moved her so. She smoked cigarette after cigarette and felt her heart breaking. That night she dreamt of a train like the one in *Anna Karenina*. She had no idea where this train would take her or where its journey would end – a train that never stopped at any stations or complained of its loneliness.

That evening as she stood at the window of her room, her forehead pressed against the glass, listening to the song over and over, she made her decision. Her studio looked out onto the courtyard where the washing and cooking were done. The evening breeze ruffled her son's little garments hanging out to dry.

The line was heavy with clothes – her delicate peignoirs and the nursing brassieres that smelled of milk and bleach. The breeze whispered plaintively and Lilith walked out of her room. Her husband was drinking his coffee on the balcony overlooking the river. She watched him sitting there in his elegant suit, his hair gleaming with health and well-being, then she gazed at the white sails of a felucca passing by on the river. She sat down opposite him silently and his gentle smile made her hesitate for a moment. She lit a cigarette to ward off the melancholy breeze that whispered to her, then she faced him squarely.

'I'm leaving. I can't bear this life any more.'

He didn't ask her where she would go or why. His reply was brief. 'My son is staying here with me.'

She nodded her head. 'Understood.'

Lilith packed her bags and disappeared. They say that the husband sent her a generous sum of money every month and that she sent postcards and photos or records and sometimes long letters from New York, or New Orleans, or Los Angeles in return. He sent her snapshots of her son on his birthdays, and later, school photographs so that she could see what he looked like as he grew up. They say that her family was furious with her at first, but that they eventually forgave her as time went by. They say that she saw her son again a few times in different cities; that she was constantly drawing his portrait; that she was studying at Princeton. People said a lot of things about Lilith, but you can't always believe what people say. Some claimed that they had spotted her in the company of a well-known bohemian painter in New York, or that she had covered her body in tattoos and taken to smoking

dope and sleeping on the streets of Harlem and went around calling herself a genius. Others said that she worked as a secretary at
a small Jewish press in Williamsburg, designing covers for cheap
books and posters for amateur theatre productions. People said
all sorts of crazy things to ease their own burning curiosity, but
no one knew the truth. Lilith tried to write her memoirs a number of times but she couldn't. Her memory had already begun to
disintegrate and by then no one cared about the truth any more.

Her son Omar came to America years later to study engineering. She opened the door and there he was. He took her in his
arms and together they tried to forget a lot of things, as though all
those years had never come between them. He lay his head in her
lap and called her Lulu. She told him all about her life, which was
no longer important or interesting. She told him how she used to
paint like a madwoman and go to the theatre and to art openings;
she said things like, 'A long time ago – before your time, Omar –
New York was like such and such.' Lilith no longer did any of the
things she told Omar about. Now she preferred to take walks in
the nearby park or to watch over the basil and wild mint plants
that grew in her window. Her son would come to see her and then
disappear for long stretches, and she would say to herself, 'He's a
young man living his life.' Sometimes he stayed with his friends
or travelled to places she knew nothing about. She believed that
it was his life to live as he liked, and she never interfered. She also
believed that time changes everything and a person never knows
what they want until they know.

The boy who had come to America to study engineering began
to experiment with acting and singing. He joined a band and trav-

elled around half the country with them. Lilith didn't notice when he started to pray all the time because whenever he tried to talk to her, she would gaze off abstractedly into the distance with a strange expression on her face. Omar began to notice that she spoke and moved about less and less. He would lay his head in her lap and say, 'What's wrong, Lulu? Why are you so far away?' If he had understood anything about the way of the world, he would have known that her soul had embarked on a long journey to a place only old people can see. There was no one to explain this to Omar and so her forgetfulness frightened him. Her son still hugs her close. He's all grown up now and married to a young, fair-skinned girl called Erica who converted at the Islamic Center in Brooklyn. He married her according to the law of God and his Prophet, and now he's a prosperous entrepreneur in the construction and demolition business and he makes a point of hiring unemployed Arab immigrants. He's also part-owner of a string of those grocery stores they call 'delis', and his partners are mostly Yemenis.

Omar has done a lot of charity work in the community. He has started giving his mother Qurans as presents in the hope that she might pick one up and read God's word a little before going to sleep. He talks to her a lot about the Quran and how reading from it regularly would soothe away her sorrows and strengthen her memory. The remedy for forgetting, he says to her, is forswearing sin and disobedience to God. But poor Lilith can't even remember her sins. He once brought her saffron as a remedy but she brushed it aside, saying that she had no need for it. And yet she does need it, and she fears this need. She fears that she will end up like the old people on the street, with dirty clothes smelling of the body's final collapse. She changes her clothes constantly, but she then forgets that she had just changed them, and changes them again. She has gotten into the habit of washing her hands every few minutes. She sits at the window that looks out onto the park, leans her head against the glass and lets her thoughts wander far away as she listens to her old Sinatra records.

Omar decided to perform the pilgrimage to Mecca. 'I've forgiven you, Mother, and I want God to forgive you too,' he said to her. 'Come with me.' He wept as he spoke. It was the first time she had heard her son say such things about her. She never really understood that she had broken his heart all those years ago and that he had lived his whole life desperately needing her to repent of it. He still remembers after all this time, she thought to herself; and then she got angry.

'So you want me to turn in circles around the Ka'ba? Son, I have no patience for turning in circles and I don't like your innuendos. You go. If He wants to forgive me, He'll forgive me.'

It was a constant struggle to stay as she was. She had never been conscious of committing the vague sins he begged her to atone for. Back then, she was still capable of living alone, of sitting on a park bench by herself and jotting down the sentences that she hoped would eventually become her memoirs in a little notebook. But she never got further than the title. Her memory rebelled against the blank white pages. She was incapable of conjuring all the little details that make up a life. She turned in circles round herself in a final, stubborn attempt to assert her independence. She pasted old photos of herself in Washington Square Park on the blank pages of the notebook. In one photo her hair is short and wild like Liza Minnelli's and her bare arms are covered in tattoos. In another, she has African braids and she's showing off a tattoo on her back that says 'I'm free' in English. A third photo shows her sitting on the sidewalk of Thompson Street, a cigarette dangling from her mouth.

The notebook, meanwhile, remained innocent of writing. She sketched one self-portrait after another in charcoal on the white pages, images of a woman with hollow cheeks and a long nose and curly black hair, hands clasped to her withered breast – a solitary woman on the threshold of winter.

Brooklyn Bridge

The hanging bridge sleeps, surrendering to the footsteps of the passers-by and the tourists and immigrants who have walked across it for two centuries or more. Small boats called ferries pass underneath it on the river that separates Brooklyn from Manhattan. Before the bridge was built the ferries were the only means of crossing to the other side. The Fulton Street and Wall Street ferries still carry photo-snapping tourists and pleasure-seekers from one bank to the other. The bridge is like a hardy old ship battered by time, welcoming the legions of unemployed on sunny winter mornings and drawing noisy activists protesting about every kind of issue, from the environment and racial discrimination to gay rights and health insurance. The processions all start out from the bridge and head to City Hall in Manhattan, and sometimes they move in the other direction, towards downtown Brooklyn.

The bridge casts a glittering mantle of enchantment over Brooklyn with all its contradictions. Hend walks across it at night for the first time, Ziyad at her side chattering away about Tarantino and the film he's about to start shooting. He laughs suddenly and Hend's heart contracts painfully. Venus has been fast asleep in her zodiac for the past few days. She marvels at the thing called love, its unexpectedness, and its breathtaking absurdity. She resolves to play out the first and final scene of her short life in the manner of a diva. As a young girl she was convinced that she resembled a few of them. She had always been a passably good actress with a talent for melodrama and histrionics. She was passionate and wilful, even though life hadn't given her the chance to express these traits to the full. When Ziyad told her that he was looking for an Arab woman to act in his short film about a family of Arab immigrants, she seized the chance to do something she had always dreamt of doing. Even when he told her that the only remuneration was a hot meal, Hend enthusiastically agreed.

Ziyad, tall and captivating, stops halfway across the bridge and tells her the story in his strong Palestinian accent. It's about a girl whose father beats her because she's forgotten how to speak in Arabic. Whenever she tries to say something, she stutters and stumbles and falls back in frustration on 'the F word' (an obscenity that means 'you and your language can go to hell'). The father, whose own dreams lay in ruins, had named his daughter after his beloved mother, and he absolutely forbade her to talk to boys. When the girl gets older she chooses a new name for herself. The father catches her kissing a boy on the Brooklyn Bridge one day. He drags her away by the hair, swearing by everything he holds sacred to kill her. At home, he forces her to take off her tight jeans and kicks her over and over. 'Whore! Slut!' he screams. Then he takes off his leather belt and beats her on her legs and buttocks as she screams in pain and fury. The police come and haul the father off, and in the last scene, the heroine runs hysterically across the Brooklyn Bridge, her desperate mother running after her and calling out in vain.

When filming begins, at first she doesn't realise that her part will be confined to one short scene. Ziyad tries to soften the blow. 'It's the most important scene in the movie!' Hend nods her head and glances at Diana Kirdashi, the eldest daughter of Abd al-Karim, who spends his days in the Arabian Nights coffee shop and distributes leaflets about the coming Day of Judgment. Diana wears a pair of torn jeans and a white T-shirt with 'I Love New York' printed on it. Hend, on the other hand, is dressed in a long Pakistani salwar kameez and her head is covered in a shawl of the kind worn by pitiful Muslim mothers in old movies. She is supposed to run after the heroine and shout 'Daughter, daughter!' with a mixture of conflicted emotions – anguish, love, fear, and disappointment. It has to show in the cast of her eyes and the hoarseness of her voice. Ziyad tells her that the shawl has to slip as she runs, uncovering her heaving breast and letting the sun glint off her grey hair.

They have to re-shoot the scene more than once because she keeps getting it all wrong and stumbling on her long clothes as she runs after her screen daughter, and Ziyad complains that she doesn't look terrified enough. He tries to explain the scene to her more clearly: 'You're a mother who is about to lose her daughter to suicide. Just concentrate your emotions on what that might feel like. Please, this is the most important scene in the film.' Hend nods to show that she understands him – even more than he imagines. But she doesn't like this role. She doesn't want to be anybody's mother. For once, she just wants to be herself; she had wanted Ziyad to see her as a woman in her own right, to see that she could play other roles than the one he had in mind.

Hend has always secretly wanted to be an actress and dreamt of playing the starring role. As a child she used to stand in front of the mirror and play-act. She would cock her eyebrows like Faten Hamama in *A Happy Day* and declare out loud, 'Shall I bring you the coat now or in a little while, sir?' She would talk to herself in a loud theatrical voice and, at the end of the 'movie', kiss the image reflected in the mirror. Her mother mocked this secret conversation with her cinematic ghosts. 'You must be possessed by demons, child, staring at yourself night and day like that in the mirror. What would you be doing if you were actually pretty?' So she spent even more time in front of the mirror, her one solace and refuge. She daubed her face with milky white lotions and stole her mother's fuchsia lipstick from the vanity drawer so that she could paint Layla Murad lips in the shape of a small deep red heart over her own. She took off her blouse and cupped the breasts that hadn't fully appeared yet as she sang her favourite song: *I'm in love and I have no regrets / People, advise me!* It was a song that she had heard her grandmother the Guest sing many a time as she washed her plastic sandals on the roof of her grandfather Muqawi Abul Karmat's house.

She put her ear to the transistor radio and repeated Shadia's lines from the radio soap opera *Bitter Honey*. The heroine was a siren who seduced men with her hoarse, lascivious voice. Shadia's voice dripped bitter honey but it wasn't as moving or provocative as the part called for. It was low and silky, and full of gentle sensuality, a dreamy voice that sounded like Zubaida Tharwat's in the movie *A Night in My Life*. Hend wished that she could escape and hide like Zubaida Tharwat in that movie – then they would miss her desperately and search frantically everywhere for her.

She would buy *Star Magazine* and gaze, moonstruck, at her favourite heroines. She tried to copy their hairstyles. She really was a great actress. Her family was constantly rediscovering this talent of hers whenever she flew into a rage and tied up her clothes in a cloth bundle and swore that she wasn't their daughter, that they had probably found her abandoned some place or other. 'Those eyes of yours are full of crocodile tears,' her mother said to her. 'What am I going to do with you? You're driving us both crazy. Dear God, instead of a daughter You've cursed me with this endless heartache.'

Radios soon become a thing of the past and her father bought the first TV set (Arab Toshiba) in all of Pharaoh's Hills. They put it in the living room between the two balconies, and Hend watched all three episodes of the wildly popular TV soap opera called *The Victim – The Departure – The Fugitive*. A group of townswomen quietly gathered around the TV in the living room, watching the show like her and crying. She tried to act out the most moving scenes, and most of the time her tears were real. She grew moody and quarrelsome, at times like a changeable breeze, at others like a raging bull, depending on the role she was playing that particular day.

When she grew a bit older, she took on the role of 'the saint'. She wore herself out praying and talking about sin and scandal. She lost weight and went around with a skinny Christ-like body covered in rags that exhibited her piety for anyone who cared to notice. She walked down the dusty paths of Pharaoh's Hills, charitably bestowing greetings on the people who lived in the cemeteries. She stood under the mulberry tree at the crossroads waiting for her friends to join her from the nearby estates, their shoes caked in mud and dust as they made their way to school. She never raised her lowered eyes for fear of temptation. During play period, she sat in the furthest corner of the classroom so as not to be noticed, shrinking into herself, practically sticking to the window so that she could gaze out at the desolate cemetery next door and contemplate sin and death while the other girls spent the whole period singing and dancing. Zuba – whose real name was Zaynab – was one of those girls. Her father had come to Pharaoh's Hills from Cairo and she was always boasting about being from the tough neighbourhood of Bulaq. She was plump and fair-skinned and she wore a pink blouse that revealed the flesh between her ivory breasts. All the male teachers constantly stared at that very spot and considered it an ode to feminine beauty. The female teachers scolded her and told her to button up her blouse, but she would just laugh her deep, throaty laugh and say, 'I swear they're just jealous of me.' The female teachers weren't the only ones. Hend was bitterly jealous of her too.

Hend always sat apart contemplating the cemetery and fantasising about a slender, movie-star figure with voluptuous, shimmying curves. Zuba carried a case in her pocket with a pair of tweezers and a roll of sewing thread, always ready to do the eyebrows of the envious teachers and students for five piastres. She sat at the very front of the classroom because she adored the spotlight. The male teachers were all obsessed with her in one way or another – their attitudes ranged from fatherly to brotherly to openly lustful. Zuba would laugh and wiggle her eyebrows at them, drawing them further into her snares. In place of a heart she had an enticing pair of breasts and she easily did without the handful of feelings that make a person laugh or cry. During informal lessons like arts and crafts or home economics, Zuba would leave the door slightly ajar and dance. She really knew how to shake her belly in a way that rivalled the infamous ghawazi dancers that Muhammad Ali banished from the city of Cairo. She pranced around and wiggled her body from head to toe. The echo of the rhythmic drumbeats never got as far as the principal's office, which was tucked far away behind the classrooms.

Why did they all envy her, Hend wondered, when she had freely chosen the role of the playful and erotic public dancer? Zuba was extremely talented, as she herself liked to say. She was an expert at waxing women's private parts and painting their eyes with kohl and their nails with cheap, flashy red polish that brought out the enticing whiteness of their hands. The 'saint' was content to observe all this with frigid contempt. She extracted a deep moral and religious lesson from the cemetery outside the window, though she knew the rumours that circulated about Zuba and the cemetery, how she charged the boys twenty-five piastres to take off her clothes in the dark between tombs so they could gape at her naked flesh. And whenever the competition between Zuba and her rivals exploded out into the open, as it sometimes did, they called her 'the graveyard girl', because the tombs were a place full of worms and corruption.

Zuba would put her hand on her hip and let out a string of obscenities. She was from Bulaq, as she kept telling everyone. 'Who do you think I am, you mommy's girls?' The girls stared at her open-mouthed while the art teacher stared at the floor in silence.

He was a pious man who feared God – so pious that he forbade them to draw human beings, or any creature with a soul for that matter. Instead he made them draw landscapes that illuminated the Creator's infinite wisdom. The art teacher didn't like Zuba and he didn't pay any attention to her, so Zuba summarily dismissed him as 'a pansy'. 'You think he's a man?' she asked defiantly. Hend glared at her. 'He's respectable and he has a romantic spirit. Not the type of person you'd be familiar with.' Zuba laughed. 'Girl, you're the romantic one,' she said insinuatingly. She knew that Hend had a crush on the art teacher and that her exaggerated interest in cemeteries was her way of impressing him with her piety. Hend didn't bother to ask how Zuba had managed to discover her secret passion. Everyone knew that the art teacher had sent her a letter in which he addressed her as 'my little kitten'. The letter had been for her alone, and Hend had accordingly hidden it in her bundle of secret papers. Despite the letter, they both stuck to their habitual roles of saint and mentor. When he talked he never looked at her. He looked at Angele – who shared her bench – instead, and said things like, 'You're a good girl, Angele. You're a saint, an angel come down from heaven.' Everyone knew his words were really meant for Hend because Angele was dark-skinned and overweight and not very attractive. The girls in the class looked at Hend with new eyes. They started calling her Mariam Fakhr al-Din, the dreamy, romantic movie star with the sweet and innocent face who trailed catastrophe in her wake. One day Zuba suddenly disappeared along with the art teacher, and rumours began to circulate that he had made her pregnant and run away with her. A number of years later they came back to the town as an officially married couple with a bunch of legally be-gotten children.

After their disappearance, Hend was filled with jealousy and shame. She wished she could hide behind Angele's huge body and shut her ears against the sarcasm and jibes of her classmates. She started to hate the role of 'saint'. She decided that it was stupid and endlessly boring and she began to try on the role of 'victim' instead. She told herself that she must be a victim, just like her mother, who did nothing but sob and sniffle and say 'yes' and 'al-right' all day long.

When her mother sat on the balcony and sang to herself, she reminded Hend of Layla Murad. There was one song in particu-lar that she would sing to her husband – provided he was in the mood, of course – when he laid his head in her lap. She would run her hand over his hair affectionately and sing: *Who can compare to him? How sweet and beautiful he is!* He would laugh and she'd contin-ue, *Marvellous spring rose, carnations, oh carnations.* He'd kiss her on the lips in front of the playing children and for those brief moments her mother would become the leading lady and her heart would swell with happiness. She sang as she cooked and cleaned and her voice rang out with the sweetness of a woman who knew that she was loved and that the time for love was, alas, too short. But when her mother got angry, she took on the role of the victim, weeping and complaining about her trials and tribulations. Hend learned her own role in life from her mother, especially after she became a mother herself. She spent her entire adolescence and youth in the belief that victims like herself had no will of their own, that they were objects of pity or compassion who played crucial roles in stories and films because they spoke to the hidden cruelty in the hearts of men and women. But one day Hend finally rose up in rebellion. She kicked the battered glass door and said to her brothers, who had by then grown into men, 'I'm going to marry him whether you like it or not' (an immortal line in countless old movies). The family elders who solemnly gathered in their white Bedouin headdresses to discuss this unheard-of insurrection declared, 'Let her go to hell, we don't want any scandals.'

She became a lovely, refined bride and her life turned into a Zahrit al-Ula movie: from now on she would play the role of the young, abandoned wife. She went back to the role of victim and deliberately courted the pity of one and all. Whenever she shut herself up in her room, her husband would say to her, 'You just can't live without some melodrama for a single day, can you?' But she was smart enough to know that he had it backward. Melodrama was part and parcel of the way of the world, like birth and death and sorrow and boredom.

In the end she decided that the most appropriate finale to that particular movie should be spectacular and open-ended, so she ran away for good. And now here she is coming down from the Brooklyn Bridge after finishing her scene and discovering the truth about her acting abilities in one fell swoop, with no make-up or lighting to keep up the illusion of a lifetime. All she had to do was run after a little whore pretending to be her daughter – the very role that she had spent her whole life trying to avoid. She thinks to herself that her life has been nothing but a series of adaptations of old movies. She tells herself that the many costumes she's worn at one time or another were never sized to fit her soul.

She remembers the red knit dress with the three green flowers that she used to wear as a child. She remembers that the colour of her school uniform was a dull grey, rather than the standard navy blue. Grey suited her because she wanted to be different, to declare her superiority. Sometimes she would throw open the doors of her mother's wardrobe and examine the flounced dresses that looked like the ones Layla Murad wore in the movie *The Education of Girls*. Her fingers lovingly lingered on the loose silky cloches, the double cloche cambered and arranged in a perfect oval around the elegant neckline. Her mother, who always complained of her aching back, no longer wore any of them, and Hend dared to hope they would be hers one day. Her mother's serial pregnancies had left their mark on her body and the abandoned dresses became a shrine to her aristocratic lineage and the days of her first slenderness, as well as a memorial to her fashionable Armenian dressmaker, who lived in Tal'at Harb Street in Cairo and made clothes for all the great actresses of the day. Now her mother was content to make an annual trip to the department stores Sednaoui and Shamla, because they were close by and their prices were reasonable. She would cautiously inquire about the price of the fine cotton linen, but she always bought the cambric printed with miniature flowers because it was cheaper and the piqué because it was tough and naturally stain-resistant.

Hend was forever taking yards of the cheap fabric to Umm Hanan. The seamstress turned them into clothes that constantly came back to her for alterations. 'Mama says can you shorten the sleeves?' 'Mama says can you lengthen this hem?' 'Mama says can you take in the waist?' Umm Hanan finally lost patience: 'You think I don't have anything to do but take care of you?' she exploded. 'Go tell your mother I don't do alterations any more!'

Her mother took care of everything – that's why Hend's clothes all looked the same when she was a young girl: modest knee-length skirts and blouses with three-quarter sleeves that would keep the sun from burning her arms but not get wet when she washed the dishes. All her blouses and dresses had to be high-necked because, as her mother always said, no daughter of hers went around with bare bosoms like actresses and prostitutes. And so Hend wore those clownish dresses made of piqué that turned her body into a neutral, shapeless thing. From time to time she tore them up or packed them away for her great escape and on these occasions her mother would say to her, 'You're driving me crazy! Are you a girl or some kind of evil spirit?'

The rending of clothes was a family tradition that she was careful to keep up, especially after she got married. Faten Hamama performed a brilliant version of this ritual in Hend's favourite film *The Thin Line*, where she played the role of a furious, abandoned woman. Hend used to take solace in the remarkable fact that even the lovely and talented Faten Hamama could play a character like that. In the end she took to wearing an embroidered abaya because she was 'the daughter of Bedouin Arabs', after all, the descendant of some tribe called the Tiyaha whose women all hid behind black veils. Her grandmother used to hang her black gowns on a washing line stretched between two nails in her room because she claimed that the moths devoured everything piled up in closets. She would point proudly to each of the gowns hanging on the line: 'Velvet from Mecca, Yemeni satin, Indian silk.' Hend never saw her wearing her Indian silk or her Yemeni satin because she only ever went out to attend the funerals of the old women in the neighbourhood. She died suddenly in her turn and the other old women put on their scented black gowns and sat at her wake, mournfully reeling off the virtues of the departed Guest. Towards the end of her life, Hend's mother also took to wearing a black abaya whenever she went out of the house on one of her rare trips to the doctor. 'Well, it's just something to cover yourself with after all . . .' she would sigh.

Hend runs her hand through her hair as she walks across the bridge. She remembers how it used to be long and black when she was a child, hiding her small skinny body and consuming all her strength. Her mother used to twist it into a single, long braid. She would get angry as she pulled and plaited the unruly mass of hair. She complained that it was like horse hair rather than human hair. Hend had no idea what horse hair was like, all she knew was that it hurt when her mother combed it. She didn't like wearing it in two braids, either. Her mother did it that way sometimes because it supposedly warded off the evil eye of the enviers. In old photos Hend can be seen staring gravely at the camera with her hair done in those two long braids. She is not beautiful. She looks out from the photograph still and quiet, obscured by the long horse-like hair that she inherited from no one. Her mother used to say that she had longed to have hair like Miss Nadia's when she was pregnant with her. Hend discovered that Miss Nadia was the music teacher who had come to Pharaoh's Hills before she was born and taught her mother how to crochet hats. She was the one who knitted the red dress that Hend always saw in the family photos, and she was apparently the one who had bequeathed her that long, ponderous mass of black hair, the like of which they had never seen in the annals of the family. Miss Nadia left Pharaoh's Hills and went back to her own country ages ago, but her name would always come up whenever the subject of Hend's hair did.

When she grew up she left the braids behind and took to wearing her hair in a huge bun pinned tight with clips because whenever she let it hang loose down her back her mother would say to her curtly, 'Gather it up.' So she gathered it up since it hid her thin face anyway. She wished she could cut it off but didn't, because she knew that her mother would then say something like, 'But your hair's your only good feature!' The men who loved her were also quite open about their obsession with her hair, and she began to hate it. On many a sleepless night as she lay struggling to ignore the painful swelling in her breasts and the acrid smell of milk that assailed her nostrils, she would suddenly realise that her baby had wound his little fist tightly in her long thick hair and fallen asleep with a blissful expression on his face. She would spend hours trying to free the strands from the vice-like grip of his fingers, but he always woke up with a start and wound his hand in the mass even more tightly. In that period of her life, her hair became a reliable barometer of the generally wretched state of her emotional health. It fell out in clumps, leaving bare patches like ulcers behind. It grew thin and frizzy as a result of her many fits of jealousy and bouts of depression, as though sharing in the wasteland of her loneliness. Her hair determined many of the roles she had played in her life.

When the Arabic teacher came back from Yemen – having

performed the pilgrimage to Mecca and repented to God – he informed her that her hair was sinful, and so she hid it underneath veils of fear. The Arabic teacher was an expert at detecting temptation wherever it was to be found: this girl's chest was too big and she should cover it completely, or the outlines of that student's rear end were too high and round under her uniform and therefore she should take off the belt around her waist and wear a loose skirt. He was quite practised at pointing out the differences between those still growing bodies. Hend covered her hair and drew closer to God. She covered it because each and every strand was sure to lead her straight to the fires of hell. She cut it short, then regretted having done so because now she could no longer recognise the girl looking out at her from the mirror.

Her hair was the battleground of many wars. She cut off a piece of it and presented it to the one she loved, a small token of her undying troth. Her mother pulled her around by it. She said things like, 'Do you think you can just let it all hang loose like that?' Hend threatened to set it on fire if they didn't let her marry of her own free will, to make her own decisions for once. She started to wear it down, in one cascading mass, liberating it from the casing of cloth and fear. It fell out in clumps after each scene with her husband. It piled up on pillows and in the teeth of combs and in the corners of her father's house. Grandmother Zaynab – God rest her soul – used to gather it into cloth pouches and bury it in the sand to protect her from the work of evil spirits once she realised that Hend's stars were crossed and that she was the object of the evil eye of the enviers. But that didn't stop her being miserable. She began to suffer from migraines. The pain emanated from underneath her scalp and the pills that she constantly swallowed were no use at all.

After he left, her mother took her head in her lap and held her close to stop her crying. She told her with the wisdom of a woman who knew everything there was to be known about migraines and aching backs and the fickleness of men, 'To hell with him, my daughter, men are good for nothing but headaches. Are you going to kill yourself fretting? Forget him.' Hend tried but she didn't forget him.

She stands gazing in the mirror at the strands of hair that fall away when she tugs at them with her hand. They lie in stray piles on the floor like a hodgepodge of memories waiting to be gathered up and tossed in the waste bin. She neither cries nor rejoices. She only feels that she's free now, just as she had always longed to be. She runs across the Brooklyn Bridge in the black coat that she picked out carefully one day from the rack in a second-hand store: a coat that expresses her fashion sense, loose and dark like a shapeless sack. It adds a few extra years and generously conceals all the things that Hend wishes to conceal. Her hair is short and black, her step hesitant, her dress modest and dignified, her gaze lowered. Some of the passers-by on Seventh Avenue mistake her for an orthodox Jew and some even hand her leaflets about Temple Beth Alohim and call her 'my little Jewish lady'. She smiles to herself because this always happens to her whenever she walks past the old watch-repair stores in Williamsburg or on Third Avenue. People in that neighbourhood always mistake her for a Mizrahi Jew. The Latinos too think she's one of them, because of her full figure and her black hair, and the Indians look at her kohl-painted eyes and nod their heads at her affectionately ('Kashmiri?' they ask her), while other immigrant communities claim her as one of their own. She walks along Seventh Avenue in the long black coat that transforms her into someone else, anyone else. She looks at herself in the mirror but can't find the little girl who used to trek past the agricultural cooperative and the Muqawi Primary School to join the dusty procession of gypsies. All she sees is a strange woman who looks like her.

12

The Cold Season

From time immemorial the Arabs have attached many meanings to the wind, perhaps more than it can bear. They took it as a good omen, but also a bad one, and they gave it countless names: the poison wind, the wind of good tidings, the lunatic wind. It carried scents across the deserts and prophesied the arrival of travellers; it warned tyrants and laid waste to villages of sin till they became like the hollow stumps of palm trees. They charged it with their dreams and desires, for the wind carried the beloved's sighs and brought tidings of the coming of the rains. They said, 'The wind plants fear in the heart of the seafarer,' and, 'The winds are hostage to His command,' for they believed that everything that happens in this world is predestined and subservient to the Supreme Will, against which men are powerless to act.

The khamasin winds descended upon the Heights in spring. They ruffled the sands on top of the hill where Hend sat with her father in front of the reception house. The leaves fell from the camphor tree and the air grew thick with dust and the smell of camphor and death. Her father said to her, 'This is the *Yud* wind.' She didn't know what the word meant, so she said nothing. 'The Persians and the people of Khurasan called it *Yud* – the wind of longing. Do you know why they gave it that name? Because of the souls of the dead. The dead constantly long for those they've left behind in this world, so they come back in the form of a gentle breeze and take away a few of their loved ones, then go back to the place they came from.' Hend was frightened. Her father went on. 'Do you know why they rub the bodies of dead people with camphor leaves after washing them?' Hend shook her head, not wanting to hear the rest of the story. For the first time, the tone of her father's voice filled her with fear, and the faraway look in his eyes made her shiver. She begged him to tell her the story of 'Hend the daughter of King Nu'man' instead.

Her father put his hand on her shoulder and they walked side by side. Hend was his only companion now that Doctor Shamil the pharmacist had left for Libya and Mr Emile the principal had gone to join his relatives in Canada. The new civil servants in town weren't interested in the reception house and its host, and most of the parties in local disputes now preferred to solve their problems in the mosque according to the laws of religion and the ways of the Prophet. Fatma al-Qarumiya had donned a long black veil and taken to sitting on the ground in front of the Nur Mosque selling musk oil, siwak toothpicks, Qurans, and pamphlets on prophetic medicine with detailed cures for such ailments as asthma and migraine. Fatma al-Qarumiya's immense body squatted squarely on the ground. She looked like a seated camel, a mass of flesh that shook when she let out her famous laugh and said to passers-by, 'What can I do, cousin? I'm a just businesswoman, I buy and sell whatever I can get in the market.'

In spite of the rapid urbanisation that had swept through Pharaoh's Hills, there were still desolate rocky heights and woods crawling with scorpions. Hend isn't sure exactly when her father started to develop an interest in the life cycle of insects, or when he began to collect with a pair of iron tongs the tiny yellow scorpions that came out at night from their lairs around the Heights. She would walk next to him carrying a fluorescent flashlight and when she pointed it at one of the creatures, it instantly froze. Her father caught the scorpions with the tongs and put them carefully in an airtight glass jar. He kept the jar in the Guest's old bedroom in the reception house. The Guest's scent still lingered in that abandoned room. Hend sniffed the familiar perfume: a mixture of olive-oil soap, musk, peppermint, and the camphor that she used to put in the folds of her gowns. When the Guest passed away her gowns grew shabby and faded, of course, but the strong smell remained, drifting out every time they opened the door to her abandoned bedroom.

Her father entered the room, followed by Hend. He placed the glass jars containing the scorpions on the windowsill. Hend stared at the wide old sill where a tray with clay water-jars and a small kerosene lamp used to sit. The Guest used to hang strings of chilli peppers, grapes, and figs to dry on its wooden frame. She often left plates of stewed beans and kishk sitting out on the sill to keep them cool and fresh. Hend gazed out at the Heights through the window, the window that let in the cold north wind. She spotted Venus gleaming in the twilight sky. The Guest used to mark the passing hours and the change of seasons as she sat at that window basking in the summer breeze, which she claimed was more exquisite than the fans of paradise. Hend stood watching her father as he transferred the yellow sand scorpions into larger transparent pickle jars, then carefully sealed them and left them on the windowsill. He shut the door fast behind him as he told her about how he was on the verge of discovering a cure for diabetes made from scorpion venom. Hend felt happy to be helping her father on such an important project, but also because he spent much more time with her now that all his old friends had gone away. They went on long walks together – from the reception house to the Heights, and from the Hill Estate back home, and they always stopped to greet the migrant workers that they passed in the fields. They spent hours every day catching spiders to feed to the scorpions. He explained his theory to her: a small injection of scorpion venom strengthens the body's immunity. He also told Hend – who wanted to believe him – that Bedouin Arabs like him knew these things because they were natives of the desert. The little scorpion farm on the windowsill became their special secret. Hend learned to tell the difference between the males and females just by looking. She had mostly gotten over her initial fear of them, until the first time she saw them mating in a weird dance that went on for hours.

It was a scene that she would never forget for as long as she lived. The male scorpion scurried back and forth, revolving around the female warily in ever narrowing circles, and they turned together in a long, cautious tango without touching. The male ejected his sperm onto the ground and the female scooped it up into her abdomen with her rear legs. She puffed up slowly, enormous and satisfied, then fell perfectly still while the male ran up and down the side of the glass jar frantically searching for an exit. The impregnated female scorpion moved towards him with slow, heavy steps, her poisonous tail raised stiffly in anticipation. The male jumped around even more frantically, knowing he was trapped. She caught him between her jaws and devoured him piece by piece, and once she had finished she fell into a long period of total immobility that lasted for days. Finally, the mother scorpion woke up. She carried the tiny embryos around on her back for weeks. After this period of gestation, the embryos were transformed into little scorpions that scurried rapidly around the jar, much like the fleeing male. They ran up and down the sides of the jar; they ran circles around themselves. They were small and hungry and terribly excited. The mother scorpion submitted to them. The little scorpions gathered around her in a tight circle and began to feed on her body. Hend was twelve years old at the time. She started having terrifying nightmares about scorpions and began to wet herself again. Her mother scolded her father sharply: 'Shame on you, the girl is unstable enough as it is and you're making her help you raise scorpions!'

For weeks after that, Hend was forbidden to join in any of her father's many projects and expeditions, from raising silkworms or hunting for black widow spiders, to observing the mating habits of yellow lizards. In the end her father failed to find his cure for diabetes. He simply abandoned the experiment altogether. He stopped going to the Heights and the reception house, and he confined himself to the eastern balcony, where he told her stories of the Prophet Solomon. He told her that when Solomon died and his soul went up to meet its Creator, his body remained behind, leaning on a cane. The construction of his splendid palace had not yet been completed, and Solomon's body stayed on to finish supervising the jinn who were building it. The jinn only realised he was dead when the ants had finished consuming his cane from the ground up, and then the body that had pretended to be living immediately toppled over. Her father died in the same way the Prophet Solomon did. One day, he just toppled off his chair in the eastern balcony. The smell of camphor drifted down from the Heights and the wind passed through, carrying off his soul and leaving his body leaning on his cane and clutching at his left shoulder in terror as the death spittle trickled out of his mouth.

When Hend's father died, her mother descended into the most profound silence. She no longer shouted at Hend, she no longer laughed or flew into rages: she just sat in the eastern balcony every evening on the wooden rocking chair, her eyes resting on the long washing line that hung between a branch of the mulberry tree and the house beam, the line that had been swinging back and forth before her eyes ever since she came from her father's house to her husband's house. On that line she had hung the silky underwear of a young bride and her white sheet stained with tears and sweat and the secretions of love. At first the scent of lavender and violets rose from the line, then, years later, the clothes that weighed it down began to smell of milk and urine and baby spittle. The line swung harder than ever under the sun, and smiled to itself.

Alone at night, it stretched out between the two worlds, keeping an eye on the balcony and listening to the stories that drifted out on the evening breeze from the rush mat. During the day it took in the smell of freshly baked bread and the leftover scraps tossed to the chickens and roosters. Her mother gazed at the lonely line, which, like her, was watching the swallows perched on the branches of the mulberry tree and listening for the shouts of the children as they ran underneath and tugged at it playfully. The children didn't care in the least whether it was warmed by the sun or tousled by the wind, and they never noticed the fine layer of dust that settled on it. Their mother sat on the balcony watching her children grow up and move further and further away from her, leaving her with long wrinkles under the eyes and minute and flexible lines on the forehead, the threads of insomnia. The clothesline watched this little woman growing old in its lifetime, each of them demarcating a space of absolute solitude. They pulled at each other, silence for silence. They watched each other intently like partners in a crime. The line would swing back and forth with its cargo of pistachio-coloured dresses and satin hair ribbons, children's socks, and brassieres stained with cancerous, clotted milk. One night, the mother smiled as she sat on the balcony and watched the old line swing to and fro; then she walked into her room and shut the door behind her, and that was the end of their story together.

✳

Hend is walking towards Fourth Avenue when the wind of longing suddenly blows up over the trees of Prospect Park, brushing against the silver and white poplars and the fragrant cypresses and oaks. Nobody usually notices the turning of the seasons in a big city like New York, where people are constantly running around, but some discerning observers will later remark upon the exceptional movement of the planets in the heavens on that day: an alignment that astronomers say occurs every forty-five years or so.

They call it *Yud*, which means the Finger of God. During this period, the planets all seem to be suddenly moving backward. It's as though you were driving a car, and all the trees on the road ahead were now behind. The trees haven't really moved backward, and the planets don't either. It just looks that way. This spring, three planets have moved backward and produced the alignment the old people call the wind of longing. Mercury, the planet of memory, moved into Capricorn, Saturn moved into Libra, Uranus into Pisces, and the earth shakes in awe at this momentous event. People wonder in amazement how all the distant memories they left behind long ago are now suddenly standing squarely before them. They cannot understand why so many things that had been erased from their thoughts are once again haunting them. The past has become the present and it is sweeping one and all away with the force of its violent return. People gather around Jojo the fortune teller on Fourth Avenue, with her ancient Egyptian scarab and her statue of a clay frog representing the god Sekhmet, guardian of the western tombs in the Valley of the Kings. And though her Russian friend Emilia tells them not to believe anything she says ('They're just a bunch of old wives' tales!'), they do not doubt that the planets now gathered to draw the image of creation have truly provoked the fragrance that fills the park with its bitter-sweet scent. They congregate in circles to watch the total eclipse of the moon over their city and talk about the stars and horoscopes and bad luck. The park has burst into flower like never before, its trees blooming with life, their white blossoms carpeting the soft ground. The scent of longing makes people fan out in groups on stoops and sidewalks and lawns and exchange greetings with random strangers. The foreigners amongst them are suddenly seized by an urgent need to talk about their distant home countries.

Narak, who had been sitting in his shop going over the accounts, picks up his violin and falls into a deep sleep. Just before he drops off, he says to his friend, 'I can smell the wind of paradise, Naguib.' Naguib al-Khalili chuckles, one eye on the lovers kissing on the green lawn and the other watching out for Lilith. He wants to tell her about things that he suddenly remembers again – the camel market, the fish market in Ataba Square, the smell of violets in old Garden City – but she doesn't come. No one has told him that Lilith had been lying in a white hospital bed for the last three days and that she can no longer move at all. She lies in her bed and says to the people standing around her, 'Open the window.' Longing blows in with the breeze that carries the smell of guava and wild mulberry and of the mastic and tamarind trees in the garden of an old house by the river, a house with a balcony smothered in gorgeous jasmine and violet and bougainvillea bushes.

She sits in a rocking chair, a small laughing child dressed in white on her lap. An elegantly dressed man smiles at them between sips of clove tea. He smokes his five o'clock cigarette before getting up to prune the branches of the jasmine bush and twine them round taut strings so that they will grow upward and cover the roof of the small villa. He is a man who likes things to be tasteful and ordered and pleasing to the eye.

Lilith closes her eyes and leaves. She doesn't watch the little boy curled up against her breast grow into a handsome young man with a wife and a retinue of dignified associates from the Muslim community in Brooklyn. They have all stood by him during his mother's illness, an illness that is now in its last stages as the doctor takes him aside. 'She's very fragile and her memory is completely gone. She might not be able to understand what's going on around her any more. I doubt she has much longer to live.' Omar Azzam shakes his head in grief and goes back to reading his Quran. He sits at the open window and gazes at Lilith's pale face. He bends down and uncovers her legs to rub ointment into the ulcers. He contemplates the colour of her skin, the marks left by childbirth on her belly, the blemishes on her face, the breast at which he never nursed. The fragrance of the lemon and orange trees in the garden of the Helwan house fills his nostrils, that fragrance that bursts forth when the delicate white blossoms carpet the ground, and he hears the buzzing of bees and sees the ghost of a young woman absorbed in a sketch of a weeping child.

As Lilith's health deteriorates, Nazahat's presence becomes essential. She is the one who changes the bedpans and takes care of Lilith's body as it lies submissive in the face of approaching death. She turns her over this way and that to avoid putting any pressure on the bed sores that have left pitiful marks on every part of her body. Nazahat takes her blood pressure and examines her urine while Erica discusses with Abd al-Karim the protocols of washing and shrouding the corpse according to Islamic law. Omar holds on tightly to his Quran and re-reads all the verses about the living and the dead as he watches his childhood pass before his eyes.

Three days later, Lilith closes her eyes forever. The wind of longing rattles the glass windows and sweeps in. It whispers to her soul and carries it far away. She goes alone, as she had arrived. The family and friends who had gathered around her sickbed now bustle about preparing for the burial. Abd al-Karim arrives with a hearse, Nazahat quickly sews up the white shroud, and Lilith's son Omar goes off to take care of the necessary documents for the burial in the Muslim cemetery in New Jersey. Then, after everyone has performed their respective duties, they all go home and pick up the threads of their busy lives.

✶

Hend and Emilia are walking along Fourth Avenue when they run into Dawij, the girl from Haiti who cleans houses in the neighbourhood. She is too busy to stop and chat but she briefly tells them that she is packing up the contents of an old lady's apartment. The lady was called Lilith and she had died a few days ago. Dawij has been hired to pack everything up into cartons and put them out on the sidewalk with a sign that says, *Take me if you want*. 'The garbage trucks will take the rest away later,' she says.

Music lovers pick up a few of the Liza Minnelli and Frank Sinatra records and ignore those of Fathiya Ahmad and Layla Murad. Some people rummage around in the boxes full of silky dresses with plunging necklines like the ones Marilyn Monroe and Sophia Loren used to wear. They inspect the satin robes, the bedspreads and sheets and pillows with Arab and Afghan and Persian-style embroidery, the Indian saris and the old-fashioned handbags. Emilia stands there with her cart, then quickly swoops down on the feast of shoes with a practised eye. She knows exactly what she wants and why. She searches for seventies-style platform shoes; pointy, high-heeled shoes like the ones in erotic movies; battered old shoes and others that no one had ever worn; cheap shoes and shoes by famous designers.

Hend pokes around in the book cartons. There are a lot of Arabic books in rare editions — *The Arabian Nights* and *The Book of Songs*, *The Prophet* by Khalil Gibran and books of Persian poetry, books that Lilith has handled and read and annotated in the margins. She turns to the cartons containing pillows and bedspreads and exquisitely embroidered sheets, then to the glassware and dresses. 'I feel like I know these things,' she says to Emilia. 'The gilded blue glass sherbet set . . . my mother had one exactly like it in her trousseau. You see this tulip china set? I swear there was one exactly like it in the silver cabinet in my grandmother al-Sharifa's house, God rest her soul. And this chiffon dress . . . I've seen my mother wearing its twin in a photo. I wish I could show it to you.' Emilia, who is busy sorting out shoes before the garbage trucks get there, laughs shrilly. 'The dead lady must have been from an Arab country — and rich!' Two Russian women pass by and exchange greetings with Emilia. One of them picks up a wig from the pile of cartons. They walk away quickly as one of them says to the other, 'You can find so many little things for free in this city — but unfortunately the apartments are too small.' Many of the passers-by stop to admire the paintings stacked in wooden crates. The same scene repeats itself for the next couple of days and people come back again and again to carry off things that they really didn't have room for in their homes. Antique dealers haul away the rarest and most unique pieces.

Hend plants herself next to a box stuffed with the papers of a woman she knew only from afar, a woman whose body now lies in a freshly dug grave. She goes through the papers and finds diaries and old photos. She says to Emilia sorrowfully, 'Why are they throwing all this stuff out right away? Doesn't she have relatives?' Emilia sighs. 'Maybe she doesn't have any kids, dear. And even if she did, where would they put all this old stuff?' Hend examines the signature on dozens of self-portraits in oil and charcoal. 'Look, Emilia, this is what Lilith looked like when she was young. Doesn't she look a little like me? Isn't that old scar under her eyebrow like the one I have? Look . . .'

'All Arabs look alike, dear – I can't tell them apart, to tell you the truth.'

Hend stretches out her legs on the sidewalk and leafs through the bits of paper tucked away in the handbags of the woman she used to see sitting with Naguib al-Khalili from a distance; a woman that she sees clearly now for the first time. She goes through all the clippings and letters and photos: Lilith, exposed to the gaze of casual passers-by. She stares at the photos of the ubiquitous Omar Azzam – the photos they had sent to Lilith from Cairo so that she could see him growing up thousands of miles away. Each photo was dated on the back (*Cairo, 1975, Mama I miss you, your son Omar*).

Hend's head spins. She looks at the photograph of a boy who is the same age as her son is now. 'Look, Emilia, doesn't this boy look like my son?'

Emilia has no time to look at anything. 'Children all look the same at first, then they shoot up and you just can't keep up with all the changes they go through,' she grumbles.

Hend lowers her head. Her dizziness gets worse suddenly and a feeling of déjà vu sweeps over her. 'Emilia, I know these papers . . .' And I know that I've written every word in them myself, she thinks. This is my handwriting, they belong to me.

'They're yours now, little one. The lady who wrote them is deader than a doornail and it's all yours now. You can take them and believe whatever you want to believe.'

Hend's voice grows more querulous. 'You don't understand. I feel like I've lived all this before, that these letters are mine, these words are mine.'

Emilia just wants to finish loading up her cart and go because it's starting to get dark. She has no time for this pointless discussion, so to cut the conversation short she says, 'You're still young, daughter, you haven't lived anything yet. When you get to be my age you'll realise that everything starts to look and feel the same when you're old. At my age everything that happens feels as though it's happened before. I know I'm getting senile, but you're still young.'

Hend sits on the sidewalk of Fourth Avenue in the middle of the boxes and furniture and lights a cigarette. She can smell the hateful odour of the milk that still burns in her breasts. She clutches a sheaf of papers to her chest, despairing of ever understanding what Lilith wanted to say. Hend walks next to Emilia as she drags her cart loaded with shoes behind her. The old Russian woman's face suddenly starts to take on Grandmother Zaynab's features before Hend's eyes – the deep wrinkles, the single tooth and flaming red irises – and Hend hears the echoing rustle of the rabbits scurrying out of their lairs and surreptitiously devouring the piles of vegetable scraps.

Emilia moves away down the street, hunched over like a weird apparition. Her parting words linger in the air between them. 'You mustn't get too worked up about these things . . . such is the way of the world . . . everything gets mixed up suddenly. We believe what we want to believe, then amnesia strikes and you don't even know who you are – or used to be – any more. We all become sorry copies of each other in the end. But you're still too young. You're too young to forget, my little one.'

Hend hurries down the sidewalk towards her house. She runs to escape Emilia's terrifying face. She does what she used to do when she was a child: she buries her head under the covers and tries to blot out her fear. In the dream that comes, the legions of identical little rabbits peep out of their lairs and scurry up the pile of clover in her father's courtyard. They nibble furiously on the green leaves, then dash back to their dark maze of tunnels under the ground of the pantry. The old women used to say that rabbits come up from their subterranean lairs to watch over the dead, that they roam the underworld eternally, reproducing themselves in the twilight space between life and death. Hend hears the hesitant patter of their nimble feet in her dreams. She stuffs a handful of hair into her mouth and reaches down to feel her underpants under the covers, wet with fear.